OS5 GRIND SYNDICATE

B S BHAMRA

INTRODUCTION

This is a gritty hard action rags to riches story with my favourite characters in Benjamin and Lucy. It starts off gritty as Benjamin is going through his teenage years he is alive and on a council estate with his family, arguments, bullying and torment of being alone, Benjamin has to wake up as he is getting more popular as he grows to know the streets in front of him. As he slowly turns his life around with the opportunity that he would never had thought was around as he grows from teenager to man as he makes deals as he gets off the streets only to find that he is the victim when things start to go wrong forcing him to make harsh decision as he loses his mind with the killings. Benjamin loses everything that he had and had learnt only to find out that he wins it all back only to lose it again. With criminal characters and running from his closet friends Benjamin is taken on a journey of crime with only his self to blame as the greed to run the streets gets the better of him only forcing him to make the same mistakes twice over. As he gathers his protection he finds that he is a wanted man with things changing rapidly goes on the run. As Benjamin travels through his mind trying his best not to lose control of his syndicate things are going wrong and he is forced to double cross his friends with a spiritual journeys Benjamin is fighting to stay at the top. Who will he trust as things are getting more on top of him with the cops breathing down his neck as well as his own posy things are getting darker can Benjamin get his life back.

CHAPTER ONE
COUNCIL
ESTATE

It is so easy to be brought in to the world and only seconds to be taken away. The streets were clean and it was late, and I had a hang over my name was Benjamin. I came from a poor background a poor family, a rough family, I was being brought up on a council estate, I did not like it. I had never had a father my father was a drunk and we just made it by, but that is not my problem I was, According to my family. While my brothers were getting high I was on the straight and narrow. I was the only one on the entire estate that was straight I was given clues here and there about what was going on I never caught on. I was to

straight and that did not help my situation at that point
but in the near future it would play to my advantage.
There was something about the people that I was
mixing with. It was like they had been brain washed.
One minute they were there the next minute they were
steeling, and then doing the street drugs as they waited
for me to take the needle. The memory was taking the
needle a sick , cowardly way to destroy themselves and
me. I had thought about it a lot and I mean a lot. It was
not for me I could not agree to there kind of pain. As
each day went by watching and learning taking each
moment of what was a good posy destroying itself for
the needle. In a way they had me but in the way that
they had seemed. I was not in to what they were doing,
as I was in and out of one of the houses which they set
up. call it a heroin house I do not know it's real name.

I was sitting on a hill top minding my own business
when I was first approached. At first I thought that I
was being be friended in fact the guy that approached
me was trying to suck me in, I was in trouble. I knew

from the very start as for his house it was a mess and it stunk of what they had been doing it forced it's way in to my brain I had no choice but to walk out

As I was alive and living on the estate it seemed at this time to be a good place except that everybody was poor in my eyes it did not make a difference until I finally decided that I wanted out, It was a decision that would make or break me in the future. I started to dream about being rich living on a council estate was living on the poverty line and what came with it was that I was living in a slum. Such things as putting the rubbish out on a daily basis and mixing with lower classes I was living with the lower classes not by choice it was a game that I had brought upon my self. I could deal with it, as I had brought it upon myself I could get out of it. I just needed some time. After I found my self on a council estate I was in shock when my father told me where I was I was only eight years of age and I was in shock. As my father had extremely high standards and I always thought that he would keep them although he seemed to think that making his life better through following me. it did not work and following me was a mistake not by me as such he had fallen for me and loved my ideas that I had.

When I finally settled down and everybody had agreed about the decision and everybody was happy and life was cosy, I was told that we had no money, so the things that we wanted had to go on hold. I was extremely up set however there was a large council estate in front of me I decided to follow suit. It was not good but it occurred to me it was obvious to me that I ws going to have to play ball with the rest of the teenagers on the estate. I ws not particularly happy, I could see it coming a mile off. It ws just a matter of time, my bigger brother knew the score and like he said that I was going to sort this one out myself. As much as I disagreed I had no choice but to agree if you see where I am coming from.

Everybody was suckered in to the same game it was dirty and I mean dirty. The only memories of the people you knew and people that you were growing up with dying one by one. It started with a bet, I was on my BMX in the court yard below my step mums flat playing as I was minding my own business I ws approached the first of my warning's about whom I was befriending. The teenagers name was Mike he approached me on his own he stopped me by getting close to me, I hit the breaks on my cycle.

" What's up man." Benjamin said.

His reply was. " Can I have a go on your bike."

I was stupid to listen to him as I got off the BMX which was mine for Christmas a present that did not mean anything as it came from my father who was a drunk and all the love was coming from else where, from his booze.

At first I said no I was now worrying as he was just standing there continuing to watch me he was not going anywhere he wanted the bike and I knew if I did not give to him it would probably be the end for me and the end for the bike. After he had asked me more than four times in the end I finally gave in. ok I said, I rode up to him and got of the saddle, and swapped places with the boy who called himself mike, well that is what he called himself I had my doubts now as he rode off with my BMX, I never saw it again.
After a five minute walk and an hour waiting for this guy mike to return I decided that he had stolen the BMX. I made my way home only to get a beating for losing the bike. Afterwards I lay on my bed over thinking as I could not get the thought out of my head. My family rubbed it in just to make sure that I had got the message. They could of stole it themselves the way

they were laughing I had no body to blame I should of not been so laid back.

As I sat down in the dinning room on the dinning table by myself I was left to think about the days events. The dinning room was small, in the kitchen there was some food it was an oxo cube in water with some carrots with some kind of flour balls in a bowl I could not eat it just looking at it was a put off I gave most of it to the dog.

.

The time came to pay my dues again this time I was minding my own business I suppose the first time I could have been suckered in with the guys politeness but this time it was different. I was break dancing on some lino just enjoying the art, music and dance. Two boys stupidly approached me asking me for a dance which in the day was called a burn. I could clearly see how it was going to turn out simply by the look at them.

As I was too scared to turn off the music and just go home. I stupidly excepted there offer of a dance. I knew what was going to happen, I wished that I had walked away. but however it was a matter of pride and they were on my turf.

And that was the way it was my very first fight with out any body protecting me but myself. After the little fight I proudly rolled up my lino, picked up the radio blaster and walked steadily and fast to my home. some how I managed to knock the two lads out. More of that was coming I could see it it seemed to me that somebody up there or down there has got it in for me.

At this point I was not really looking for god but in the end I had found him it was not by choice it was my fathers doing. I complained almost immediately as nobody else in the house had to learn how to prey. I had no choice I was being drafted, sold in to the church. I had to go to Sunday school. I was not particularly happy at that moment not because I had been put in front of god but I had been put in front of god with the wrong clothes. I remembered clearly second hand shoes which were two sizes to big and flairs. My mum was dressing me up on purpose to make me look stupid to embarrass me. even my poorest friend was now dressing better than me. somebody had to tell her I was going to church not that it made any difference I was still treated as a second class citizen in my own family.

MOVE

I had finally hurt somebody which gave me the idea
that you cannot trust anybody, going back to the fight
which was in a near by wood. People can be un trust
worthy. People can be devious it seems, from that point
I refused to trust anybody. I was pretending to do kung-
fu outside in what other teenagers called the square I
was minding my own business when I was approached
by two extremely small people they were about my age
and I knew the both of them from school. They were
my younger brothers rivals. John and another mike,
they said that they were looking for him my brother I
chose not to answer them and I continued to play fight I
could see my brothers future I was pretending to fight
and he was going to have a fight. After they had
questioned me on what I was doing they kindly moved
off. I was thinking that they had it lucky. I was about
five inches taller and a little stockier but that was not

the end of that particular situation within a few minutes
I was surrounded by the rest of the kids on the estate. I
could not believe it john and mike had told everybody
what I had been practicing. As I tried to explain.
"look it was nothing. I was just pretending look it ws
nothing. Look I cannot fight I am a fairy."
As I continued the conversation I was surrounded it
would be just a matter of time before one of them hit
me. I was ready as I held my stance continuously that
all I was doing was pretending to fight.
The lads in front of me did not bye it and some of them
were some of my friends when I look back at that
situation it breaks my heart.

All in all there was eight maybe nine of them. I knew
them all by name and if I did not make a move quickly
I knew that I was going to be on the receiving end. I
was still waiting for them to return my football which I
had with me as I went to snatch the ball back
 They were content in passing the ball around
themselves expecting me to jump and complain I could
not do anything so I kept my cool. I knew that being
cool was a good answer for peer pressure I got it at
school all the time from players and not fitting in.
fitting in with friends would soon come on that account

I could see everything I was waiting for the ball to be thrown back to me it did not happen what happened was that one of the lads booted the football over the high fence that guarded the court I was told to fetch it instead I went home and thanked them for the route it was an easy escape however I never saw that football again. My seventh move was to scream and shout at the top of my voice at all of them and give them a sign, it was probably two fingers at that time. As I did I bumped straight into the old man. I was not expecting him and not knowing the time as it was now dinner time. As he took me by the ear. Probably just for the sake of hurting me. as he dragged me down the stairs questioning me why was I late and who was I verbally insulting, I guess even an old drunk could keep me polite and in my shoes apart from the pain of him pulling my ear I guess he could have been a better father. As he dragged me down the stairs through the door and into the living room not shouting but speaking quietly hard and soft questioning what I had been doing. I knew if I had told him the truth it would of escalated.

took a deep breath telling him what did not happen my family were the type to start a neighbourhood fight that was his pride, as I continued to put the blame on my self as I just about made a half true story up, as I put the blame on myself. That evening I went to bed with know supper and no wash. As I curled up on my bunk the tears slowly came to my eyes I was thinking while I cried that there had to be a better place than the one that I was in. in the end is all I did was cry my self asleep. It was one of the hardest decisions to make that I was going to run away. it was not the only solution and it was playing on mind a lot. In the morning I was at school on this particular day it was going to be my day off I was bunking. The plan was to hide in the wood and I could spend the rest of the day in the country side counting grass hoppers and playing around.

As I danced around running up and down old hills that were bent and dashing in and around large trees, that is when I noticed it there was a tree swing a blue rope and it was tied to a black tire I approached it I was not alone as the swing was swinging as I approached the swing after climbing up a small ledge reaching out to the rope that I could not reach I found that I was disappointed as I could not reach it. I could imagine that fun that I could have had. I was again rather disappointed. I tried again with a long stick to hook it and bring the rope in and tire in but with no luck. Even with the stick I was still to small. Better luck next time I thought. I continued to play, running up and down through old bunkers scaring the grass hoppers and chasing the butterfly there was a lot in the fields in the end I dived in to the long grass gasping and holding my breath whilst timing myself.

I was thinking about the time of year it was as I presumed that it was now spring but in fact it was now summer that when I had lost it but only for a few minutes. As I tried to figure out the mathematics of it all I sat back and closed my eyes with a long piece of grass in my mouth. There was a peaceful feeling about the place it was like everything was perfect it was as if I had been here before. I was trying to keep my mouth shut I wanted to stay in the wood but it would have been silly as my watch was telling me that it was home time I left the wood just in time to get behind the school kids that were passing by. I fitted in perfectly, keeping my head down hoping that the older children did not notice me as I was walking with them. the last thing I needed now was another fight, a school fight. Most of the kids were normal but there was always someone bigger then your self, as I walked through them trying to find the right year. I would sense that some body would see me. I moved quickly. This time I was lucky but felt like a coward for ignoring some other pupils problem as I bumped past the older teenager in my way with my head down and looking onwards just happy to get past them I made my way home lucky with no scratches. I was reasonably upset and disturbed, as I got in to the house it was silent I asked my mother where were my two brothers she had said that they had not arrived from work yet. I knew that it was bullshit. They had gone to the cinema I knew that they had been at home as well as I walked past my brothers jacket in the hall way I did not take it any further and all I wanted to do at that point was to cry. As I had been left out again I went to my room and cried my self to sleep I was obviously upset as I looked around half asleep I was hating my room one I had to share it with my brother and it was to small as I pulled my duvet up closer to myself up over closer to my face. and rapped around my body to feel more comfortable.

I lent over on to one side closing my eyes and chose what I was going to dream about as I sat in my mind thinking it was nice to be left alone simply to think at that point I awoke quickly as somebody it was my father shouting his voice or should I say sounded like the drunk that he was, it looked like he was getting a grilling again for being to drunk. I did not feel comfortable however within the hour it ws over and I could go back to sleep.

According to the mind and I did not know this at the time dreams only last a few minutes and mostly occur in the morning. Probably as you wake up what is bothering me is about that is that I have never seen the end of any of the dreams that I have had and on top of that every time that I was having a dream somebody would always walk in and wake me up. I found it extremely frustrating that I had never seen the end of my dreams.

As I knuckled and buckled my self into the bed I was preparing myself for an epic adventure through my mind wait, I was not on any kind of drugs just the power of thought I now believe that I had stubbled across something it was not my mind, I had begun to think not just to think but to explore the mind.

Planet beat
Chapter three

As my mind raced once I was asleep I found the perfect
place for myself it was in a place of peace. It was in
planet beat in the world of rock the world of rich
people. The world of TV , anybody who was anybody
would be there, even the movie stars. It was like a large
hotel but with an extremely large party and you had to
be a member how you would become a member, it
would happen through your mind. And if you got in
you would know. On the first night or should I say early
morning I was excepted simply as I had the dream I
was gifted when I awoke in the morning I could not
believe it I went straight to my mother and tried to
explain it she ignored me telling me it was just a dream.
After she had drummed it out of me that it was not real
I was so upset that she did not believe it and from that
point onwards I keep myself to myself I did not tell my

brothers until later I will explain as for my father he was to drunk and looked at me making the crazy sign telling me that I had lost my mind. At such a young age I tried for weeks to explain and everyday they all just sent me to my room. My brothers and family were just laughing at me behind my back. It was not nice being the middle mad brother. By my brothers mouth he had got the whole council estate laughing at me. Not face to face but again behind my back, as we played football it was the way that they were looking at me I had noticed all of them made the sign you know the one.

I was being given the loopy sign, I knew that they all knew, I was reasonably upset set and went home straight away I had to have a word with my brothers except when I got home and they were in front of me they looked a little bigger than I had thought. I walked in to the lounge even before I had a chance to approach them he told me to get out of the room in a bullish type of manor that was to start with I stayed put and he could see what he was going to provoke, I held my ground but I wanted to attack him weather it was going to be verbally or physically in the end it was verbally he was not a safe person he was a little bit harder than me as he was older I had a chance to make a move as he raised his voice trying to scare me I charged at him running up to him my face in his face I probably will not do that again.

As my brother yelled out at me I yelled back at him I shouted " Why did you tell every body about my dreams."

His reply was that he thinks that I was a crazy person and everybody should know and nobody want's to hear my stupid story's about mixing with the stars. Or my weird dreams about being an actor.

My brother did not know his words at that point, he had broken my heart. I hated him more than ever more than our dad.

As I walked out of the room the tears begun to swell up and one tear just fell I in to my palm some how I managed to catch it some thing weird was happening the tear crystalized, that when I knew that I had not been dreaming and it was true. I waited for a second to walk back to my room where my younger brother was standing my consciousness sent me back to my bunk. A knew game had begun.

As I walked away from my older brother my youngest brother was around me giving me some support I was having to protect him in the ways that he would protect me in the future I did not want to lead him astray as I had been myself with the dreams that I had been having. In the end I sat down with the whole family on a movie night and tried to tell them everything they would not listen and the conversation with what I was trying to explain did not convince them that I was sane in fact they thought the opposite I had found myself a concrete slab they told me shut my mouth just shut up and watch the movie. I refused as I wanted them to believe me and again I was hit by my mum who then hit my brother the older brother who sho0uted out the words what was that for, who then hit me and broke my nose. I ran out to the bath room crying and yelling you have broken my nose, my nose after I had cleaned myself up and made it back to my bunk.

I could not of had a worse day, first arguments then the fighting I went back to bed I had woken up early this time I did not have any dreams and as I got up early I had to make my breakfast with out permission, the cluttering around must have been heard from upstairs as my mother came straight down stairs to tell me off my argument was that I was just getting my breakfast. My mother was acting like I had robbed the place if it was anybody else she would have said nothing it was just the fact that it was me.

After I had a large bowl of cereal put back in to it's box Benjamin walked out with an upset look on his face he was angry and wanted to scream, his mother was becoming another brother and not the mother that she was.

Benjamin went to get dressed not knowing that it was the school holiday's as he gets dressed and is ready to walk to school seeing no students on the way believes that he is late. As he climbs the steps that lead to his front door, as Benjamin prepares himself to leave his mum calls him Benjamin has no choice but to listen quite clever as Benjamin finds out that it is the summer holidays. Benjamin reply is that she could of told him before he had got dressed he throws his school bag down on to the floor and polity asks his mother for some money there's a pause and then silent. Benjamin is given twenty pence he closes his hand turns around and walks out, still dressed in his school uniform.

It was not was expected but says nothing in fear as he doe's not want his mother to take his money back he heads up to the street to the sweet shop as Benjamin walks it looks like everything is in order except his mind his imagination he just started dreaming of money.

By the time I had been in and out of the shop the thought of making money had left it had disappeared for that moment and the thought had changed to sweets. Twenty pence mix up were Benjamin words to the shop assistant Benjamin eyes lit up as the sweets from the jar were pushed into the small bag and handed to him, Benjamin took a slow walk home taking everything in mostly his surroundings. Benjamin liked adventure as

now it was getting close to Benjamin's birthday he
chose to spend it in the wood talking to grass hoppers
but it was to come a few days later and he was waiting
for the right time to enjoy the thought. This time he
thought that he would take a milk bottle from outside of
his dads flat and catch some of the grass hoppers bring
them back and show the family. He had an idea already
that they would not be interested anyway. But he did it
anyway.

As Benjamin lays in the lake of tall grass he closes his
eyes and listens to the grass hoppers he can hear them
well and he see them the sound of the backs of there
legs rubbing together making noise like a war chant.
Benjamin is at peace and at one once he catches one he
goes ion to catch more continuing his hunt another and
another knowing that he can only have them to study
for a short time before he has to put them back once his
bottle is full he takes one last look at the wood,
Benjamin does not know yet but he is obsest. The rope
is still swinging and Benjamin wants to play. He says to
himself.

 " if only that I was taller."

As Benjamin is still to short to reach the swing he turns
his back on that account and walks out of the wood.
Passing the horses paddock and makes his way home.

Benjamin is curiously looking at the grass hoppers they
had stopped making the noises he knows that they
wanted to be taken back and freed but he is content and
consistant in talking to them all the way home. he takes
them in side trying to conceal them from everybody he
goes straight to his room to study them. Benjamin is so
intrigued by his new friends he mises dinner and the
game was up Benjamin was sent to take them back
Benjamin could of guessed that outcome he was

thinking now at this point if he should re turn to his home as he knew that he was going to get told off and probably grounded or even worse a black eye from his brother. Eventually the sun sets and the summer sky dims and the clouds move and the darkness settles in. Benjamin is found out side sitting on his mothers doorstep he is called in side by his father who was already drunk and sends him back out side not to dwell but to go to the shop the off license for beer.

Benjamin real thought s were to tell him to go himself but Benjamin was scared, and he knew that he should complain, he was bound to get into more trouble and end up with a slap and no supper to go with it. Benjamin closes his eyes and takes the money from his dad not being concerned with the thoughts he goes outside to finish the chore Benjamin was thinking differently towards his so called family. He would never get up set he just did what he was told even when he got things right he always seemed to be on the receiving end. He only meant to do well. As the darkness set in for the winter I had a few ideas of how winter was going to make me some money, well pocket money, I suppose you could call it was my guy that was made up out of my old jumper stuffed and a clown mask I stood in the street shouting and asking people for money people would walk by I would on purposely ask them for change. I would say penny for a guy. This was not the only money making scheme that I had up my sleeve there was also carol singing and Halloween At the end of the day I would have hoped to make a few pounds I closed my eyes grabbing the guy and picking up the money left on the floor. I was on my way home but first the sweet shop. Nobody in my family realized that I was business minded when I tried to speak with them and tell them what I was actually doing they were not interested they left me to mine own cause.

This for me was as I was only just nine up set me they did not care I wanted to get out I wished that I would get my revenge I had decided that I was going to run away where was the question I did not know anywhere would do. The question was how was I going to do it it was going to take timing and strength it not everyday that you plan to run away from your house.

I was in the park sitting on a bench trying to figure out how I was going to make the move I mean run away it was not as simple as it looked again I closed my eyes thinking, trying I was really pushing my mind for solution's and ideas, in the end I just gave up and walked home as I neared and needed my house I was in time about entering and approaching it I knew straight away that I was un welcome. I knew as soon as I had walked through the door that I was going to be bullied weather it was my conscious that had lied next door or if any brothers had

I hated everything about the place. As I was trying to understand family life I was no expert in bring myself down my brothers kept on telling me to wake up. I never saw the same side of his story he never made sense his thought s left me confused only because he thought he was getting something out of it. He realized that it was coming from my mistakes he thought that I was making in fact they were his.

waterloo
chapter four

I was down and out I had decided to leave my home,
leaving my parents was the hardest thing that I could do
brothers and sisters too. I was leaving my family it was
at that time good for me it was a good thing but a bad
decision looking back on what I had done in the past.
Leaving home in such away that I did I had done it
before twice when I was a teenager anyway I knew that
could turn it around. All the talk and how bad it actually
was. Was coming true, no more parties no more friends
as they could see the danger, I could not that was my
mistake. As I sat down at waterloo station reality had
begun to set in. things were beginning to bite. There
was no turning to mother now. As I watched each train
pass by wondering how the people manage to stay with
it.

The commute everyday getting up doing the same thing
everyday, I guess that is life. As time went by more
people started to notice me in my case that was not
good, all I wanted to do was to keep a low profile I did
not want any body to notice me but the ticket officer
did that one discussion that one thought had destroyed

me I could no longer stay where I was as I was comfortable, after a short argument the police arrived I did not want to tell them anything. This part of my life was waterloo as soon as they had thrown me out I was back this was going to recurring I had no where else to go. I did not want to go home. as educated as I was going home meant nothing to me nobody actually cared I did not want to be drawn back into that kind of life. I was not that kind of guy that wanted to be bullied I was not asking my parents to pick me up the tab as such I wanted to make it and I wanted to make it on my own it was my own fault nobody to blame but myself.

I sat down with my sleeping bag and a blanket it was not the first time that I had been on the street. In fact it was the second I cannot remember the last time but this time felt easier. I pushed my sleeping bag in to a corner of a door way I was not looking for hand outs as I had enough on me for the moment it was just the circumstances. I was in a position knowing that I had put myself in the position. There was nobody to blame. I said those words again to myself as I shuffled down into the sleeping bag. My first night on the street. As I laid there in the cold night asleep. It was winter I had began to dream. I was going on a journey. I was not impressed as I new already what I was going to go through my mind where I was going I could not tell you. I believed that I was going to the a city it was called the city of Lou.

As I awoke as I sat down some how I must of stood up and stayed there with my eyes closed in the cold only to stop the cold from reaching me I began to travel through my mind as I was traveling through my mind I was thinking that this was going to be a lesson learnt. The that I was on started of slowly I liked it at first but as time went on I began to pick things up new things which were addictive and putting it down was becoming harder. Once I had studied it the journeys that I was making became easier for me at that time. There were times I would just close my eyes. I would just take my self there with no problems although this journey had a bad part like every story has a good start and a bad ending I was meeting people who I did not want to met and it was if they were controlling the journey for me instead of me. I was trying to avoid them but once it was done it was done . I wanted to come back but there was something in there system which had trapped me there. I was forced to stay . I was trying to open my eyes to wake my self up I was so tired so the journey continued.

As time went by quickly I was learning things of the street anything and everything that you could imagine steeling, drugs, corruption by the time I was sixteen I nobody could touch me. I had given my secret to my very best friend and I did not trust him in fact I did not trust anybody at that time. In the end he double crossed me and I knew that he was going to double cross me. he sold me out and was giving all the money that I had made away dishing it out he told a few other people and the word went out from there.

You know the posy the word was out that I was dealing I was not a happy man as the school days past I was getting more weird looks I knew at that point I knew at that point that I suppose you could call it noticed within a few weeks after I had sat my last exam I was out anybody who was anybody who was in the school was taking a hit. They were now addicted.

Unfortunately I was the one that was not getting paid my best friends had sold me out, believing that they could make a profit. I suppose they would call it justice I looked at it as being alone if you could excuse the expression.

As time past I healed all the thoughts of telling one person that I had found what I had found and what it had changed into. A dry drug dealing business. As I dreamt my mind to better places that could be thought of by me. no body could enter my mind or find me. I was finally healing and was feeling good again about myself, it had taken a long time a few years I did not look at this as a mistake the mind can be a big place. As my friends started taking control of my business I was now on the losing end of things I could clearly see were it was going I had decided that I would leave them I was going to leave the posy. I had better and knew means of making income at least it would not be on my mind. I did not believe in what they thought and I did not believe in what they were doing. They were out of control and they thought it was cool they did not know the real out come. And it was me that was going to have to bail them all out.

I did not like and they did not like it. I believed that I had an excuse I had no family. There excuse was that they were using it for personal use. I did not by it and I do not think anybody else would.

As the pressure began it was coming slowly again and again the same old compliments at the front door day in and day out it was typical, I need you to score for me, rubbish, I did it for them any way just so that they would go away. this was only the start. I had spent a lot of time thinking where all this business is coming from. I was rather popular the old bill knew about it which meant I was in danger. It was funny you know but I felt as if I was being watched if that makes sense. As I walked down the street the same feeling occurred again this was the first time I took it personally, it was nobody I knew, as I kept on looking over one shoulder it was a knew experience for me.

Back up

Chapter five

After all the arguments I was beginning to think that
family life was a waist of time for me I could not see
what my brothers had claimed to see. even through the
forced thought . I had lied in telling him that I could see
the question was what exactly was I suppose to see
even mo0re so what did he see. As I laid in bed one
evening he found out that I had lied I had lied about

taking the drugs that he was giving me he forced upon me, I ended up with a punch in the face, lesson learnt do not lie to your brother.

I needed some serious therapy it was like everybody was watching me as I closed my eyes the life that I was expecting was becoming the opposite. I knew that I would not be able to tell anybody the true truth it was to hard and things change. My life was now a mess, spiritually and humanly I had nowhere to run to. The brother that I was running from ended up in a nice new home. the home that I had found again I found my self in the dark instead of the light. Where was I going to run to next my brothers did not know that I was dealing drugs. As each and everyday would pass, I would be silent hiding my secret. I knew that I could not tell anybody. but that was going to change but not yet a few years down the line. I will explain later.

As I laid on my bed dreaming of all sorts of things including money how I could suck the life out of everybody that knew that I was on drugs. It was like a game it was becoming a game. A game that I did not want to play. It was personal, in fact it was so personal that even though I was in I did not want any body that I knew to know as I was using it for medical reasons. I was stupid to make a deal one that I would never forget. As I pushed the mistakes I made as a teenager aside nothing I did seemed to help my situation. giving some guy his first hit would remind my life as words of myself was now going around. That

child that teenager could not keep his mouth shut. And before I knew it my whole business was known, I was up set.

I could see my future top kid in destress as the plans to deal a whole school had been blow out of my hand, before I had a chance to explain it was all over the school. I could of cried over that mistake. It only take one person with a big mouth.

As time went by I was becoming more and more unpopular due to the fact that I was supposed to be on the inside I was now on the outside. Instead of my clients coming to me they were going to him. I was thinking and only thinking I should paste him in front of everybody in the school play ground. Except I had no back up and it all fell on my bottle.
It was going to be tough decision as I had no back up it was just going to be me. it kind of reminded me of a TV programme it was scary and exciting all at the same time. Even more so I was just about to earn my respect. But in fact the whole thong had worked in reverse I did not see it coming but I was fast enough to be aware the first chap that approached me laid in to me while we were getting busy and I was fending him off his boys started.

I wanted to take them on in fact I did not have much choice as I picked my self up off the ground I was on it again they were talking as I picked myself up off the hard concrete floor
I could feel the blood running form my nose and out of my mouth I had a busted lip also. After they had finished I got another punch in the stomach as they said good bye. I was not particularly up set but spiritually it had hardened my heart. And I wanted to get my own

back. I went home if you could call it that. A council estate I could not remember the actual name but it was totally horrible. As I walked the balcony I was thinking that I had to get out I needed a plan away of escaping this poverty that I was in the poverty that I had to get away from the poverty that I was having nightmare s over.

As I walked towards the front door of the house I could close my eyes trying to tell my self that this was not happening I was just tall enough to see over the balcony there was not to much to look at. As I walked in to my home I was greeted by my step brother another victim another user. And then my step mother I really thought about that one. All I wanted to do is stay away from them for being poor even more so thinking poor. The reason was that they were sucking the class out of me my brothers a man I once call my father. I needed to make a phone call. I could leave quickly and make it look like I had just left. I left my home I was on the street it was better then being beaten up and left half starving.

Chapter six
One minute thirty
seconds

At last I thought that I had found a girl that I was going
to marry. I was not in town I was busy on a business
trip when I got a call. My girl friend was holding a
party of course it was on my behalf.
Although the more I thought of it I was beginning to
think that she was playing around. She was holding a
party while I was away.as I put the phone down I could
clearly see what she was saying the relationship was
over. It was obvious, then came the questions why was
she telling me that she was holding a party I could not
comprehend the whole situation the phone call was
enough it defines the whole logical feeling's of the

mind. I mean you do not ring your boy friend when he is out of town and tell him that you are throwing a party do you.

The game was getting dirty every time I had helped some body another problem would create itself it was like I was being forced but it was me. I was to generous and I knew this however business was business. At that point I just sated over again I was making money lots of money. People on the street had started to pay there respects. As my business went from dealing one friend if you could call him that to next and then to the next I had established a business a drug dealing business with perks.

I had them robbing for me it was a dirty game but business was business. We were not just looking at drugs but girls , sex, drugs, cars anything that we could find, nick and sell I had started the syndicate it was not by choice it just happened and it happened fast. I guess it was the sign of the times that is the way I look at it. As the money rolled in I am not talking thousands I am talking hundreds of thousands I had everybody including the geeks they were the best.

It gave me great pleasure watching the most education school boys, the boys that took the piss out of us for being better educated than us as screwed up as me now they were just the same as them. but a little, just un educated what ever I did they thought it was cool, honestly how thick can you be.

So with all the excitement and having I suppose you could call it a syndicate things had started to flourish I was no longer a drug dealer I was a business man. As more of my friends started to approach me I started giving them names. Daniel the dog, mark the car, Luke and Luke they were named as they were twins, noodles, there was some other guy who ws up for it needles theses were my players all heading and looking for the big time. As it goes as much as we had discussed it we would always help the poor.

And they pledged that they would never cross each other although strange as it may seem I had my syndicate. All Benjamin was asking from them was that they would be honest.

We were all getting rich and Benjamin was loving it he was loving and watching every crime yet he had not committed one yet himself. Benjamin was taking kindly to being followed how he was managing to stay alive he did not know I guess it was luck.

As I closed my eyes I could se everything the future and the past. As time went by things were looking good and I was surprised of the loyalty that I was being given even though I did not trust any of them. lee was beginning to get on our nerves I had a number of complaints about how dirty he was especially his clothes. Dirty suit and un polished shoes he seemed to forget who he worked for everybody seemed to think that he was a waist of time and space. The syndicate wanted him replaced I disagreed once your in you are in for life.

I needed a break away from the boys, I had a feeling that it was going to be a short one and it was. When I got back everything was in a mess. I should of not trusted myself not to of left the syndicate we had started losing business.

Business moves quickly and we went from the top straight to the bottom from having everything to having nothing and I mean nothing. No food, no houses, and no money. I was extremely up set. I closed my eyes and I was looking for answers. But I found none. I was told through a decision that we should move find a new place the competition was to much it was the only answer that I could find.

It was a solution I was not particularly happy about it and the syndicate was not happy either. I had to put everything that I had thought about that morning and explained the situation to them in a meeting. The people my people were not happy. I was given one minute and thirty seconds to speak and argue. It was probably one of the hardest things that I had to do as I stood our game was over there was some tears and some anger they were upset with my decision.

Aft6er a short meeting the posse disappointed disappeared and I made my way home. Benjamin pulls out a smoke expecting a cigar, out of his jacket pocket he lights it up knowing to keep quiet, as Benjamin trusted no body which included his driver. He smiles as he puffs on the end blowing out the smoke. Benjamin puts his hand in to his jacket pulling out a gun Benjamin thinks that he is being followed, he tells his driver after getting in the car for a short journey to pull over. The car behind him pulls over also Benjamin does not mess around he does not wait he calmly and quickly gets out of his car and asks no questions as the driver of the other car behind him he walks towards it opening fire sending an a ray of bullets into the standing car. After taking a good look at it he gets back into his car he tells his driver to drive.

As it came to my thoughts I had nobody left, Darrel would come over now and again he would question me as we sat talking about anything and everything that would make me feel more calm. We discussed the past and the present and the future I was keeping the syndicate quiet I knew that if I was to slip up it would be the end of me.

It was funny looking at my situation I had not committed a crime as such as yet I had been caught in a different way a spiritual way. But Darrel he was something else I was meeting with him maybe once or twice a week and we would talk about the same stuff. Still leaving the syndicate out of the conversation it was completely clear that he thought that I was completely nuts. You know losing my mind each session was getting harder for me to hide the truth.

At the end of each session I would say I will leave it at that.

Things in the business had began to change I found myself in a new position a position of being conned, new people had moved in forcing the poor to move and most of the people that used to work for me to leave the playground. In normal terms they were buying my men. It did not take long before more street gangs moved in it was not long before the street wars had started and other gangs moved in. All I could think about was that was mine that was my plot. In fact there was only three but three was enough, to take control of the council estate there was he Russians the Indians and the blacks and then the whites I could see it so clear exactly what was happening what was going on even though I was frozen out, I was kind of happy I was just glad that we were not in Mexico and they were not anyway. I could close my eyes again as I sat in the jacuzzi with my pistol by my side it was getting to dirty for me I wanted out.

Chapter seven
No business none of your business

I needed some leeway as I needed the time and space to tell the boys that we were done and the game that I was playing was over everybody was suited and booted as we met in the normal place and I had to give them the news. The syndicate was over, done and destroyed I told them that the new street gang had taken control. I had a hefty pay check enough for everybody to live satisfactory. The boys disagreed and complained saying it was none of there business now. Benjamin continued he knew it was a hard thing to do and they all should except it he says again it is over. He said polity I promised them that the syndicate we will be back but it was going to take some time and all of them should be prepared.

I did not think that any of my boys were really interested in the money they were to brotherly and acted like it. in my eyes that was a good thing. It actually brought them and formed them a family everybody stuck together it was my home it was my syndicate and I was going to miss them. The last day came slowly one of the girls said that we should throw a party , I was not that convinced and I wanted things to run smoothly, normally. Although it was put across to me a couple of times by other individuals . still I stuck to my first decision and still refused to celebrate the end of our business.

I said no. there was a few complaints, as I told the guests not to push it our time in this part of the city was finished it was done. I had lost my temper over the last conversation I was shouting that it was over when I was found as I watched the sunset from my window I was still thinking of how.

How I was going to bring them all back there was a lot of people depending on that one decision I could clearly see the way it was going to end up.
Everything was peaceful at that moment I had a chance to relax, no police no body had approached me for days making me belief that I was having a free ride and I was to go unpunished a fee ride. Until there was a knock on the door it was one of mine it was the dog as I opened the door I greeted him.

47

"HI dog."
He replied hello
" what's going on."
Mark the dog." Not a lot."
He began to question me quite a lot he was asking all
kinds of questions I had to tell him to slow down it was
an overload of questions and some of them were
unanswerable. In the end I had enough as I snatched up
the beer that I was drinking of my kitchen side and
throwing it at the door.

As I took over the questioning and asked him why so
many questions his answer to that is that the boys
wanted to know. I did not want to express my true
feeling at that time. It was a hard time for me. As he left
with no answers some of the other boys began
The word was that the boys my boys were beginning to
worry and they were now on my doorstep too. I had to
tell them the same and I could see that they were slowly
losing there faith.in me. this was getting on top of me.
slowly as I tried not to hit the bottle, it was weird
suddenly being at the top of everything being at the top
of the game then suddenly being dragged back down to
the bottom of the worlds greatest stage, as I closed my
eyes I could see everything, weather it was a gift or not
I could clearly see that it was real nobody else actually
knew it was late and all I wanted to do I could think
about the boys I owned them. they all had respected
Benjamin.
As I awoke after a few hours in my mind not sleeping
just standing and some sitting and leaning in the
doorways I opened my eyes.

As I did I found myself in a totally different place I
closed my eyes immediately and when I opened them I
was back. However when Benjamin closed them again
he was taking back again however when I opened them
a again I was back to the second place again as I finally
settled down I found myself on top of an extremely
large building where I was I did not know. It took me
quite a while to settle down. The first thought that was I
had been talking to the wrong people and I will be true I
was scared. I called out but there was no answer. As I
stepped closer to the edge that's when it happened I
heard a voice.

"do not get to close."

I chose to listen to it I could not find any other normal
answer. It sounded like a man. I had begun to enjoy the
sensation it felt good, even though I already knew that
what I was experiencing was not real as I was using my
mind to shape the surrounding area I was learning
quickly and even though I was in control I was learning
new things quickly. I kind of had the feeling that in was
un new York. However that had left me a slight
problem as I lived in London and I had never been to
new York. As I looked at the city 's sky line the sun
was setting I was thinking that I could get used to this.
It was a frill.

How and why this was happening to me I did not know it was an extremely weird experience I could not explain it and I needed to visit it again. As I tried to find it as I travelled I got nowhere everything was quiet the only sound that I could hear was the traffic passing by. In the end I disregarded it as a dream, but it was not. As I laid on my bed thinking about the boys thinking about everything that they had been through. Thinking about the experience that I had with them. I began to regather my thoughts if they existed in the first place. Somehow I manged to say in there long enough to find an answer. I managed to find another place. If possible a better world. Not for them but for me. It sounds a little crazy, I had questions why? And funny enough I got an answer it was our way back it was the only answer that I was given I had been given a gift it would give me the chance but how would I explain to my syndicate it was going to be complicated the first thing I wanted from it was my boys back., all flush the second was our business and the third the streets. It was like I was making a deal with the devil but in fact it was quite the opposite it was more like god. As I continued to go through my mind it felt like I was controlling things I was dreaming I started wanting to be in other places it was like I was being controlled it had taken control of me I had locked myself away I was not answering the phone and I refused to answer the door. I had stopped eating and I was wearing the same clothes I had been I the same pants for months. It had taken over me I was convinced that I was in control of my people as it was in control of me and the things about me especially crime on the streets. On seven occasions I had the same dream there was a bank heist it was my boys I was controlling there every move. I was watching and controlling them with every thought I could see everything.

As I saw visions and I was getting used to the new game I began to speak through things that I did not know I began to hear things that were not there and I

could see things that seemed to me that could hear me
at one point I was given the instructions to me for one
of my boys he did it I was surprised I was an
uncontrolled thought in my own mind. It had been wees
and weeks since I had spoken to anybody my whole life
had changed this was a new game I closed my eyes
again I could see my self on a beech no body around I
was at the sea side in the cafe drinking a cup od tea. I
told myself to spill some into the saucer
Then I told the waiter for the check and that happened
also it was to hard and to complexed to understand at
this moment what was spilling the drink I must of done
that for a reason.
As I brought my self back it was painful I mean really
painful I ended up on the floor in a lot of pain after a
few minutes I was fine again and back to my old ways.
I was beginning to think that I could control the future.
As I came out of the future I came out of the vision I
could hear her words as I closed my eyes once more
again I was taken to the same places over and over it
was like a scene not from a film or a music production I
did not know the thought had escaped my mind it was
or I should say it felt extremely real to the point that I
could now feel the people and see the people I was
greeting people as I was watching there crimes.

I closed my mind as I was traveling meeting people dreaming the things of the future I found it very interesting as I was finding answers to my problems it was like I was in with god. Everything that I asked for ,it was done I did not understand it fully as I was given I was thinking what would I have to give back once I was done in return. The answer to that was nothing. At that time god was playing a big part in my life. I hope you and him understood.

I was being the gangster that I was I always I knew my self and I had to know where I was coming from the boys did not see it, they seemed to be half way. They had not questioned me and they did not know the way that I now was. Thinking about it kind of made me feel sorry for them as they were stuck in the old ways who was he what was he doing and most of all who was controlling them. it was not me I would have told them if I was I was to scared and I left it to them if tat makes any sense they all had to make the decision they were told that they had two options they were to stick with me and god or they can turn away and do it alone.

After I had been thrown off the plane that I was going to travel on there was going to be a fight with all the men. Looking back at the situation I was in shock for a few moments later I opened my eyes it had begun I needed a safer place as I knew that I was in danger. The power of money and the thought of being even more powerful than I was in the first place and the power of money to go with the thought I was so rich I had began to see the future. I had nowhere to run to I had nowhere to turn to no more friends I was on my own I had gained a gift although it had saddened me to see that I had lost everything.

And knowing that I had lost my friends hurt a lot.

I walked to my fridge and opened the door it seemed to occur as I pulled the beer out of the fridge I downed it all at once I took it the manly way none of this sipping stuff. I was looking up at the sky's they were darkening quickly there was a defiant presents in the room there was a change in my mind it changed from a yellow to a morbid blue I was surprised as the colours changed. As I opened another beer and took a swig from it the clouds changed again. I could see it clearly.

As I went to sit down on which was now a heavenly sofa slowly putting up my feet up on the foot stool I was thinking about how I can get out of the gloomy apartment. I thinking who could I turn to. I remined myself again over thinking that I did not have any left. I wanted revenge and I was going to get it. it was only a matter of time at that point Benjamin realizes that he had a lot of time on his hands. With all the confusion he loses his temper as he throws the empty beer bottle across the room and smashing it on the floor Benjamin is focused on the bottle as he sits down watching the beer slowly drip on to the floor on the tiled surface. I needed some time to think as ten killers is all I could think about. Benjamin words were how the hell am I going to get out of this one he counts again on his fingers. Benjamin knows that they were looking for him and it was not as if people did not know his address. It was obvious that Benjamin was going to have to move and quickly and alone where would he go who would he turn to I had to leave this very evening he did not feel safe.

Within that small moment of frustration and I had become paranoid, I locked the front door and it had begun except not in that order that I explained earlier after having a couple of out bursts I picked up my car keys I was going out for some fresh air and a drive totally forgetting what he had just experience within the two hours and totally forgetting the warning. Benjamin walks straight out of his apartment in to the building doors . he walks to the lift reaching out with one hand presses the lift button top floor as the lift arrive he steps in side there sis nobody around as he stretches out his arm again pushing the ground floor button which was called gf he settle down in the lift and awaits to be taken down stairs. The lift is moving down wards and Benjamin slowly forgetting everything that he had just experienced. Only to wake up as the lift stops suddenly at the bottom of the building. The computerised mechanical vice tells Benjamin exactly where he is first floor Benjamin waits a second presses the button once more ground floor. He waits a moment the lift moves for a minute and Benjamin is underground in the car park the lift doors open and Benjamin can see his car from inside of he lift he walks out. The lift doors close he see them as turns his head. He checks his pockets for his car keys. The car park was quiet the images that Benjamin had seen were coming back to him as Benjamin remembers what he had seen through his mind I guess it could be real as he approaches his car. A car screeches Benjamin knows it was to fast to fast to be a passer by.

I had only just stepped out of the lift and the car sped towards me then coming to a halt then reversing backwards then forwards careering towards me again, I pulled out my gun and I took aim I did not fire the car drove off but past me probably to get a good look at me. I was not the man that he wanted either that or the weapon that I had had warned him off. A minute later another car appeared to me this time there was no warning it was real I was not one for waiting around in aa poorly lit car park underground it was unreal being in my position everything at that moment had slowed down. The light seemed a lot dimmer I could see everything clearly what had caught my attention was the ceiling and the darkness of it in the distance. As the car approached he knew exactly what I was seeing it was exactly what I saw in the vision it was perfect I closed my eyes moving quickly behind some park cars,

I pulled out my gun I was still scared the adrenaline helped a bit but was not enough the car again sped past me I could clearly hear the gun shots there was a mistake there was no where to hide

I was not a where that I was suppose to be shooting at it I just looked at it and fired my gun

There was a return of fire I moved quickly to my car I was thinking at last. Getting in it very fast, not forgetting that there was two of them and not one I had lost sight of the first one as I approached the car park. I could only think that the first car would be waiting for me probably outside they probably knew that I was armed and making my way out of the building. I put the keys into the ignition the engine started I reversed out of the parking bay out on to the hard concrete leaving extremely fast up and out of the building I was right they were waiting a car chase had begun.

As I shifted the gears first, second, third, and forth. I was driving fast over the speed limit only to draw more attention to my self there were cameras everywhere it was not like I was going to go unnoticed.

As I was now behind him instead of me being in front of him and closing in distance we met at the traffic lights I came to a complete halt it seemed like the right place I opened my car door stepping out on to the concrete road as I slammed the car door shut making my presents known. As I drew my gun and casually walked to his door drivers side on the left side I seemed to be in the right place I tapped on the window stupid move he wines down his window I did not have to think I shot him three times mark the dog was dead. I stood there looking at him for a minute as other car had slowly pulled up what I had done was going to give me some kick backs I did not know it was mark the dog that's all I can say. As I watched the blood pour from him pour from his dead body cramped and slumped over the car steering wheel.

One down nine to go it was a shame that it was either me or mark the dog because he always seemed to be a nice fellow. We were friends. I had to put him in a place of peace. All I can say now is he should of listened he would have been better off.

I was not sure weather they were following me if they were I did not have any idea of who they were going to send next. The guy was clumsy using his own car I was tough enough to pay him a visit my self in saying that it would probably happen. The colour of the car and the number plate was a give away it had mark the dog on it he was probably one of the strongest people I knew however he was nasty and that is why he was one of the weakest he was weak as he was one of the weakest in the old posy.

Why I called him dog I do not know I was the one that named him. As for loyalty goes well here is the answer he really sucked at it. I knew at the end of the day I was

having to go and kill him the only difference is that he
came for me instead of me going to him.

After the death of mark the dog I decided to go down
town to drown my sorrows. Some where down town out
of the site of people. I found a bar it was dirty the whole
place stank of beer and used women it was totally the
place that dog would hang out in that last comment
made himself feel worse it di not help the situation as I
just killed the man with that name. As the evening
went on the only thing that had not happened was that I
had not picked a fight. That thought, I was surprised
that it did not happen when I said it I was in luck
because everything I have said in the last few days has
happened god must be looking over me. As I said that it
started happening as some guy was acting like a jerk it
was obvious that he had ran out of money and he was
trying to buy himself a drink verbally. I should of put
him in his place as I did to mark the dog.
As I took another glass of whisky knocking it back
hoping that it would numb the thought of being me only
that I would see the next part of or should I say the next

victim I decided to leave the bar I had nowhere to go, I sept in my car.

The only thought left was to drive and the last thing I needed was a fine for drunken driving but I got into the car and drove it anyway. I did not care where I as going I was heading out of town as I drove out of the city un a where were I was going not knowing that I was being followed all I knew at that point was I was heading out of town.

As luck had it I had given up the road and took the bus as the bus had distinctive destination like the mind. It was extremely late in the evening and I was surprised that the buses ran all night. I was in the right place as the driver drove me to destination to destination I did not know were I was going to end up as I checked my clock sending a spiritual message to myself I suppose you could call it intuition there was going to be some action. The thought was where I took this seriously extremely seriously as I looked out of the rear window the there was a car I kept my eye on making sure I could always see it. they had found me they were tailing the bus it was obvious.

I asked the driver to stop the bus he began to ask me why and he could not as there was no parking bay he continued that there are rules he asked him again this time I raised my voice.

The bus driver asked a question. "why."

I just told him I wanted to get off the bus as I managed to convince him he pulls over I was expecting to wait he drove off leaving me in no mans land. The car that was following me continued to drive past me I had got that one totally wrong. I checked my gun magazine for precaution it was full I was left to walk seven miles or so to the next town once I was there I was looking for a place to stay. I was pretty cool about the whole situation I thought I was out off danger but in fact I had walked seven miles in to my own murder. It looked like I had a friend waiting for me.

Every thing I saw was like a vision it was like I had been there before in the building everything that I had seen it was to real. The first thing that I had noticed was that the room that I had been given was on the top floor. The second was the man how did he find me but he had, it was the guy called needles somebody must of tipped him off. Before I had a chance to approach him he had approached me he came out to be quite polite conversation saying how nice it was to see me I could see right through him and his polite gesture of offering me a drink at the bar if I was lucky I would be able to keep him there all night.

It was clear to me that he was going to get me plastered it would be easier for him to stick the knife in. I knew his weapon and I knew exactly what I was going to do. As he ordered me more drinks. Sat that point I thought that I should decline I was thinking at that point that I would just play along I also noticed that he had stopped drinking as I was now plastered nice and drunk I had

61

been drinking well into the night and into the early hours of the morning he was surprised that I was still standing as I closed my eyes for the first time, I was pretty drunk totally forgetting why I was there and what I was suppose to be doing. It all came back as he asked me to walk him to his car.

I could clearly see what he was trying to do, I could see his alibi for me that we were both drunk which gave him the upper hand, I saw the next vision. He would say he did it when we were fighting even though I was armed which he had removed while I was drinking I had to make a decision before we both ended up dead as we both walked to the car I felt him prod me in the back with my own gun what he did not know I removed the bullets before I had entered the bar he did not check the magazine. It was quiet enough that was better for me as any noise especially a gun would heard for miles. He was about to grab me he was two yards in front of me I would of shot him except he had the gun I had the magazine as he continued to talk I said nothing I just looked at him straight in the eyes. As I was his old boss you would of thought that he would think that I would know his moves. He picks up the pace a bit trying to

make me think that he was in a rush. I was following him slowly watching his movements,
I closed my eyes somehow I knew all of his movements in one thought. The first he was going to make a phone call the second he was going to remove my arm the third well there was not one because by the time he had drawn his gun I was one step a head of him and had drawn my gun and my gun was a silencer that means no noise it would hardly make a sound my number two was needles he was dead.

I stood the looking at the body he was still bleeding when I lifted up the body and removed this ID. As I removed his wallet as I was looking for something that would tell me who were they going to send me next. I was not the kind of person who enjoyed running away from my problems there was a saying instead of them coming to you I would go to them. in my mind it seemed easier. Lazy and incompliant to the rules of assassin.

At that point the thought would not remove itself from me, which was a bad move I could be found though thought it was simple the things that people receive on a day to day basis messages that are there right in front of them and they do not see it would be just a matter of time before Benjamin understands not many people do it was telepathy basically

And there was a twenty to thirty level of it that was only a guess I am not sure in reality.

Needles was now dead and the news travelled quickly before I knew it they had sent me another I told you that it would happen as I tried to explain to them what was happening as I raised a meeting there was lots of jokes about it all I needed to do is win one of my old boys back and the rest would follow. I was trying to tell them that they were all being used not by me I was in it as much as they all were I was the target doing all the killing I was as in much pain as they were it was obvious that they were being sent to me because they knew that I would kill them and then I would be the only one left. The other street gang and my own street gang would all be dead they did not by it I was up set I was free to go my own blood was yelling at me hide Benjamin and do not come out to play. For some strange reason they had let me go probably out of respect. I was expecting somebody to try and make an attempt but I got nothing as I stepped and drove off fast in to the country side I pulled over and waited there was nothing not a sound I was in the clear.

It was late and I was drunk I was in three worlds or it seemed like it. one I would blow my head off not my style but still a thought two swallow a jewel and choke to death and three find the next guy who was going to make an attempt on my life. In fact there was a fourth they had found me and had entered my mind. Somebody had tip them off, I was to make a move although there was something that I needed to discuss, it was the police it looked like they were in on it as well.

I saw an image just a glimpse as I thought about the bigger it became. At that moment I totally turned my mind off and put everything to one side I did not know what to think about it. it seemed to me that some so called police officer had been sent to me for some stupid reason she was a detective she was looking over me she was my back up. I do not know what kind of premonition that she had been having but she was really laying in to my mind eventually I had to let her in. She used brute force she felt good I did not like good. She was going to take a little while to get used to I could tell. I reminded myself that it works both ways so I told her to be warned. She disappeared again meaning that she had gone a sleep probably had not slept for days and days like I did went first found out.

On the other side she was talking I could hear her clearly this guy is making me feel dirty he has forced his way into my mind he is having a good time. I have asked him to stop but it is continues. The girl was good at getting in to Benjamin s head.

As time went on they were still watching me the more that I tried to forget it the more they would come for me. I had nothing to hide only that I had been in touch I knew exactly what they knew and the police had started to play my game.

It was late when the worst of my fear were slowly becoming alive the cops were there, they seemed to think that I would notice them, I did.
As I closed my eyes I could feel everything it was David a cop and a snitch we went back years I do not know why he could of left thigs the way they were. It was the opposite the first message that I had got was

that he had got it in for me. when I heard the message I cannot remember who from and right now that is not important, I was not bothered. The guy was slim, I could do a better job than him.

I closed my eyes again even though I thought it was a good they were always there to rearrange my situation with them, as soon as I was on top of things my business they would come strolling in. they were trying to bring me down that was typical os5.

I began to hate this man as he freed himself in to my mind telling me that he was here to ease the pain. Telling me it was by my family.

This police presents in my life was not what I wanted and as he was a cop I would have to put up with him for now, I was upset. As time went by it moved quickly I had got used to my new friend in my mind I was taking a battering constantly as I fort to take control the constant entering of my mind by this one person was slowly destroying everything that I had built. When we met I still did not understand him I was at that time I was trying to put the thought behind me in fact the opposite happened

" You are not as famous as you think".

 were his words. My reply to that was.

 " More famous than you think".

He still insisted that he was my friend all I wanted to do was to shut up and go away. later on in that day after telling him the way tat I had felt he continued to play the same game that he was somebody that should trust as I opened my eyes in surprise then closed them again Dave was in my mind and on my journey instead of me I was not up set as I did not want to know him, not now, not ever.

When I closed my eyes again he was gone there was no
sign of him, in the end I just put it down to paranoia as
my mind was looking for its next victim to make an
attempt on my life. As it goes I was still in my mind
watching them they did not know I could see
everything the robbery's, the killing, it was weird I
actually began to think that the things and the way that I
was brought up was a waist of time. I was actually
shocked. I ws about to change my attitude. I was
becoming straight again according to my self. I had no
boss because I was one as I tried to except it and it was
not that hard. The posy had a different point of view
somehow they figured out that I wanted out.
That was the new posy the old pose the white dragons
as they renamed themselves after we had split they all
believed that I still wanted them, with me, they had no
control and I was not going to offer them my services
like I said before they had no control.
The pressure was now on I had the old posy the white
dragons trying to insult me and now that I had some
new boys they said that they would protect me. it was
not the sat of the story.
As I closed my eyes as I was trying to get away from
the whole thing the opposite had happened I ws
dragged further in and I did not like it. the whit dragon
and my new boys.
I was tired of the argument's it was late I decided to
take a walk out side it was unusual   for me to do that
but I needed to clear the air the over load of thoughts as

I was trying to think for a solution. As I past the parked cars reminding my self of how we used to do it in the old days. The memories flooding back, it would not take more than a few seconds to break in to the cars that were in front of me, take off it's wheels not for money but for respect it was the things that I can do if anything else I would turn a blind eye while it was being done for me.

I still had the old posse watching me the last thing that I told them before I had left them that they should look smart there was a lot of opinions and arguments over this.

I needed to see the future that was my only thought again. I told myself that needles was dead and I had killed him after I had left the body on the street and waited in his car keeping a low profile as the cops turned up. After watching them lay the tap up and closing off the road and area. I stayed low but close as I was watching the proceedings, no body saw me and no body said a word. I had seen enough I had already removed the dead guys car keys, wallet and everything else that could connect me with the murder. I took the keys off the dashboard, as I pushed the keys into the ignition and wiping the inside of the window screen off clear so that I could still see mostly everything that was in front of me I slowly pulled away hoping that no body would notice me mostly people in front me hoping that the engine was not a loud one. I drove off to a safer, quieter place. As I drove off unnoticed as I wished I said to myself.

" Three of them had gone who will be next".

I was driving and I was in deep thought, it did not feel right driving a dead mans car. Even so I put up with it it actually smelt like him.

I had drove to find another town I could not mention the name as I did not know it. the smell in the end was too much and I pulled over it was coming from somewhere in the car for a moment I thought it was me, I took my jacket off folding it and raising it my face it was not me I grabbed the car keys quickly and walked to the back of the car. As I pushed in the keys to open the boot it was a body and it was a dead body. Who ever it was had been suffocated . Needles must of known that he had it coming in doing so he had left me a dead body, within that second of thinking I had lost my temper dead body's are not the easiest things to deal with. It was quite serious.

I was shouting at god who the hell was why did he do this to me and such things likened to that. What was I supposed to do with it. of course I had to play the game it was not easy getting rid of dead body's taking in to mind that I had just left one six foot under. I wanted to know the name of the dentist I pulled the stiff out of the boot not caring about it. that alone was hard work ,digging a six foot whole was even harder. As I dragged the body over to it thinking what I had been I hope I had not had to discuss this with any of my children. As I pushed the body rolling it over until I came to the edge of the grave I gave it one more hard shove and it

70

finally fell in. I did not know the victim at first, I had a list in my mind of who it could be.

I was thinking for one man this was to much and that I needed a holiday. The whole thing had taken me three hours the pit that I had dug was not on holy ground so I spent a few minutes saying a pray.

It was probably one of needles girls that is what it looked like to me it looks like he had left the end of his dirty work for me. Needles was a dirty man not in habit just dirty in the way that he did things. I was happy to see him dead. As for the other girl in the boot of the car I did not know her like I had as before just another victim of my syndicate. One that should not of happened as our laws say what come around goes around.

As for my new brothers I have decided that there would be an argument in the way that they were to dress. They were confused and actually unhappy, I did not care. I told the white dragon that it was time to go and smarten up. I told them that if they wanted in they would have to wear a suit. That is trouser ,shirt ,and jacket and a tie if they had one and if not they will come to me for a hand out that would be returned to buy one.

After along discussion they began to bow down to my offer, I held my argument until everybody agreed finally, they did. It did not take me long to convince the boys I was back in business. Although I was still upset about how much time it took me to convince them. there was lots of questions mainly about loyalty as I had to explain to the point that I was having to threaten them. if they did not listen they should leave and lose a finger. after I said that there was quiet they now knew that I was serious, I was reasonably happy and told them that the meeting was over. And everybody should go home. they did and I was left alone again.

Os5 peace keeper
Chapter Eight

The time would come when the boy's would muscle down they knew that I was there target and it would be an act of loyalty it worked both ways except I had the upper hand it all decides on weather there was anybody out there. who had the bottle it would only be a matter of time. As I closed my eyes again somehow welding this gift a gift that I did not want a curse when I looked at it I was still making up my mind. If it was actually doing anything for me. all I know is that I could see my future. I did not have time to experiment with it was slowly taking over me and I was finding it hard to except the things that I was seeing. I did not think that my friends, brothers and people were so easy to convince and two faced I did not judge them as much as I wanted.

I used to think that everybody was normal I always thought that I was high profile for a while anyway I was a lesser power as there were things above me that were bigger, even though with all my boys on the street made me feel like I owned the them. in a sense I felt reasonable normal in my mind I knew people were talking that did not make anything easier. And with the constant meditation left me believing that I was at the top I could not reach ant higher. Little did I know as I explained.

I wanted revenge I had been out of town to long but there seemed as soon as I got there it sent a sent I was like a dog and they were little foxes as I decided that I would spend a couple of nights on the streets hoping that somebody would know me. As paranoid as I was there was better places that I could be. It was like a game of chess and I was the last piece it was that last move as I was dreaming about a chess game when a car pulled up the window was already down, I told them to leave as I was stuck I did not need anybody I ws in control I was just hanging out the driver that I spoke to understood me and left.

If and when the boys hear that story as I was mistaken by some guy as a call girl I was sure that it would bring a laugh and they would be talking about foe quite awhile. Any way thinking about the boys I had better things to do. As they knew that they had to kill me that I am sure was enough. As I found a place to dwell in a old doorway I closed my eyes instantaneously the images were there I was recovering bomb blasted the future to my mind at this point I was sitting down in the same place as I pulled up the coat and blanket where they came from I do not know, but it was a disguise as I did not want anybody to know that it was me. As I went on unrecognised, as the evening went on the people were tossing coins at me, and people swearing I will not repeat what was said and it ws not once or twice. I could hear it all the homeless were not particularly liked in this part of town which lead me to believe that the homeless were not liked at all.

I closed my eyes again once more this time blocking everything out of my mind I had no idea where I was at that time and I slowly fell asleep. It was good to be back I was feeling like my old self. I had no idea at that time what I was playing with and I needed more time to experiment, I realized almost straight away that I could not approach anybody. not even my closet friends as I had seen images of their truth in my mind.

After spending the time on the street I chose that I should dwell in a more secure place and found my self a hotel knowing that it was a god send after spending time out on the street.

Everything was at hand as they were preparing to make an attempt on my life, thinking nothing of it. I needed another break as for burring needles and the dead girl as well I had left the hotel and went off to find another. I was worried which was un usual for me I had miscalculated time and things I did not feel any better. As I bumped in to my next victim lucky for me unlucky for them.

This time it was easier than the last it was like the old days the way we approached each other sat down at a table I did not particularly want to kill him I just wanted to put a bullet in this leg. As we both sat down he ordered me a drink, I was thinking he was going out the same way needles did. I did not have to ask, his movement were more than familiar.

It was not as if I was going to have to pay for it myself, he was flush as I was, the guy that was on the bar and there was an unusual amount of people in the bar. In one corner the bikers and at the other end the guy trying to make a living singing I had an audience as much as he did. That was something to think about.

As the night went on I slowly was figuring things out the first question to myself was why did I come to the bar, I never got to ask the next question as one of the boys walked in.

Shouting my name out as loud as the music its self his words were.

" I want Benjamin dead".

As the man opens his leather waist coat showing everybody the bomb which he had tied to him. As the crowed opened up a catwalk for him to walk down they looked in shock and were as scared as me. as the crowed whooed themselves away not realizing the impact his words were as I heard them ten times over. Still shouting that he wanted Benjamin . Benjamin walks in to the space that had been created by the crowed before they had moved in fact the hotel had it's drinking bar down stairs it looked and felt like an underground carpark and it also resembled one. In fact it was one there seemed to be lots of cars there Benjamin had not noticed. As Benjamin closes his eyes waiting on a solution he finds nothing and has to use roll play he was disappointed and a tear came from his eye the man who was threating was one of him. Why had we changed I do not know. All I do know is that he wanted me and himself dead.

As we moved closer together as the public moved and departed out of the underground parking he could not have chose a better place not only that he was in the position of killing me but he could take out the whole building. As he moved closer with a gun by his side in his hand openly showing what he had attached to him. I called out to him some body had to make a move. I could clearly see that it was ED.

Benjamin " ED".

He calls back " Benjamin".

Ed replies " You know you are a wanted man Benjamin".

Benjamin " yeah I do". There is a pause but only for a few seconds. Benjamin continues.

You know that you do not have to do this."

Ed " I have no choice."

Benjamin could see the pressure on Ed's face it did not look to good. Nobody had called the police which made the talking even harder. The small conversation continued.

Benjamin " What ever your new boss has said please ignore it I can find you somewhere safe."

Ed was not buying Benjamin's sweet talk it looks like he has other idea's. I did not want to kill Ed however he was leaving me no options, as he moved closer to me literatly a few steps, he pulls the switch, it was a dud somebody had set him up. the package that he had had been re-wired. It did not work , for that moment I fell everything I had done seemed to rush in to my past through my mind, but I had no choice and I did not believe in second and third chances I lifted up my weapon from the inside of my jacket pushing it against his chest not even thinking twice about I shot Ed and now he is dead. I could feel his pain as it became mine. I took his soul with me and god knows it. I knew that I could walk away as I looked back as I looked at things I was thinking that the victim was not me. but the new syndicate and old pals kept turning up. while double crossing me somebody wanted me and at the end of the day I was hoping for a little more respect. I knew that the boys had double crossed me and they were coming for like a baby to candy. As ED and Needles were dead and the strange body in the boot of the car still had no name as yet. I was thinking again I was thinking that their new boss had it in for me next as a few weeks went by I had heard nothing and seen nothing.

There was no guns fights no brawling and no attempt on my life I was thinking that they had forgotten about me I was a little less surprised when the forth member of the syndicate arrived polite as usual I did not even think about what was going to happen. I had seen the images over and over as he approached me.. Again I called for the barman this time I was buying the drinks, it ws like something like out of a western film. I would order the drink's the bad guy would refuse and then I would tell him again but the other way around then we would both step outside, the barman would duck behind the bar and the anybody else would run and hide. It was that scene.

Benjamin thought. There was a pause, Benjamin stopped outside only to be believing that it was going to be the end of my life and the end of fate.

As the two gangs that were running and becoming more and more well known I decided that I would go back. Go back to my old business, I did not want to I would hope that it would look like I had given up. you can understand the that it started as only a thought one that grew. A thought which would come to me a lot. I was trying to push it side it was not easy, I woke up on my bed I was sleeping alone it was a single bed all the partying was over for tat night. I was alone only the birds and the wind was not there to disturb me. as it was the evening although their was one sound which came to visit me once every evening to entertain me I asked myself what was it looking for was I going to die. I looked at the thought over was there a reason for this I was feeling paranoid as I was trying to wave the thought away. it did not look like I was going to be able to escape. As I manged to take control of the situation and the long thought that I thought was not going to leave.

As I sat down on my chair in the bedroom thinking I was bombarded with thoughts some good and some bad I left the room in a state of confusion. Knowing good and bad.it was as I predicted I was not sure what to think I did not know weather it ws pain and pressure again I closed my eyes when I a woke I was trying not knowing at this point at this time I did not know who I was to make things complicated who was I.

I was the peace maker that I what I decided to call my self I needed a new name anyway that name like it and it stuck with me, I was happy that I was keeping myself happy even though I had my troubles. The next attempt on my life was that I saw was that I was thrown out of an apartment window this did not help knowing that the people that wanted me dead just knowing that I was alive just knowing that I was living up in the penthouse sweet.

As I was thinking I stupidly walked to the windows looking closely at the penthouse door s turning my back still stepping backwards as I thought that it was along way down to the bottom. As I closed my eyes I could see everything in motion there were three things coming to my home., then the argument then nothing I did not see the actual out come I could only imagine that I had escaped some how once I had looked at these images I sat down believing that I had one that I was on the winning side, my side.

I did not think at that time that it would happen, exactly two mi9nute s after the premonition. There was as knock at the door . being cared I chose to ignore at first. But the knocking did not go away it got worse.at this point I lost my temper as I stood up facing the door it was to late the bullets started flying I had already produced my gun and was returning fire as the bullets few ripping my door apart I was telling myself that this was the end I could not see the way out of this situation and if I did not I was asking if god did

Benjamin continues under fire.

Benjamin" do as your told and say your preys sure that going to save me, tidy your room you will be a better person". This conversation with Benjamin continues as he cannot see away out of the situation that he was in he thinking of god and saying a few preys as he went along he preferred it with god by his side.. As the two men eventually and rather quickly kicked in Benjamin's front door. I was in the position to open fire again on them it was now my turn which quickly became there's again. Upon fire I gave then some verbal abuse I was saying thing's like this is my town in doing so they returned more fire it was like something out of a movie things such a walls . doors, floor . the whole of my kitchen and even the ceiling there was not a lot left and I was lucky to be alive. I eventually got a new magazine in to my gun I was still under fire as bullets ripped through the pots and anything that was steel in the room mostly kitchen wear. I returned fire accordingly but could see know body's then there was silence, nothing. Then a small clicking sound they were reloading. It was a reasonable large apartment and I had a few idea's as I new the way around it played to my advantage. As I moved around I told my systems to turn the lights off I could fight better in the dark.

Once the first decision was made I had decided to move in the first assassin was dead I moved quickly finishing him off with a couple of bullets to his chest I thought that it would do he was wearing a vest as I looked at him as he stayed put on the floor I removed his bullet proof vest and looked at it I had him pinned down as I put his vest on there was no sound again as I signed him the hush sign I did not kill in cold blood he was out for the count I made sure as I had knocked him out with the but of my gun. The next guy was a little bit nifty it could not have been made any easier as he was checking his partner over I had two clear shots he was fast but not fast enough. As he saw me in the reflection as he turned around the game was on as he raised his arm in a position saying that he had given in. and was trying to talk me out of what I consider to be a good position. I was trying my hardest not to talk to him he ws trying to draw me to him. I closed my eyes hoping that I would see the future mine and his. I got nothing. As I opened my eyes he had gone,

I was on my own, I was thinking that he was probably behind me in the gun smoke that we had both left. I turned quickly. As I walked off in to his direction through the smoke it was still rising through the walls and off the floor all I had left as I looked d at it as I walked around looking for the second assassin.

As I found him with ease I hit his body I knew this as I was right in front of him as I looked downwards with my eyes upon him he had no one to turn to h had nowhere to run. I refused to raise my gun but gave him a huge thump which left him unconscious on my kitchen. The third target was the first target as he awoke I did not hit him had enough he was still looking around my home for me and the second target.. I knew the way in and the ways out of my pad so I did not have a problem finding things especially un welcome guests. I knew that he would follow me outside as I had his partner with me I had taken a hostage I was outside I made a little time to re load as I did one handed while still clinching the first assassin with my freehand. I was counting the bullets as I put them in. one, two , three , four, five , six. All in and ready to use. I knew that the assassin would follow me outside when their people wanted some thing they would normally get it. I had his partner but in thi9s case his brother made by respect not by birth by one hand, this is were the word comes in to it. I stood there for one more minute I let go off the brother and I leapt down wards of the ledge there was no talking deals, there was a pool below. As I hit the water I hit it harder than I thought I shattered I was fighting as all I wanted to do was yell. I held my breath under the water there was very little light which was better for me I was under the water holding my breath I knew how fast they could move it was not going to be long before they find me. my presents in the area was still felt as I was drawing them both to me again. It was not long as they were coming closer I laid under the water holding my breath as they looked for me shouting at one each other.

As they got closer to the edge of the swimming pool it gave me chance to destroy the both of them I could them both looking but un a where of what they were looking at. I unsubmerged myself out of the water opening my arms as he was turning away he sees and realizes that I was there all the time as I fired into him two bullets he fell into the pool backwards we had swap places. I was now wet but on dry land as I stepped out of the pool. He was in the water there was a loud splash.

Leaving the memory with him rather than me, that's one more dead as I continued to calculate the death toll. The only thought that I had in my head was who was going to try me next I could make an educated guess. I went back upstairs to check the damage picking up the cars keys on the way back down. I walked to my car I drove back to the hotel and made the arrangements to have the place fixed I hated being with out a home. I wanted the streets to know that I meant business. I told my butler who ws taking care of my home if he was questioned about anything just make something up and we would deal with it later.

He was told not to mention my name.

I told my driver who saw the whole thing from the car to get back into the car I gave him the address and told him to drive me there. at this point I could not trust anybody for now I knew that I was wanted dead I did not know where I was going on that account I gave new directions to my driver somewhere out of town He did as he was told I was at a loss not really thinking everything felt weird it was if I was dreaming things seemed to slow down I closed my eyes again sending myself well back not realizing who I might meet or where I might end up. The game was not just creeping up on me it was creeping up on everybody.

I told my driver to take me to a safe place I did not have to go home in fact I no longer had one fit to live in. as we drove my driver was questioning me it was like he needed to know I told him as much as I could I told him straight that the only one that asks questions was me he appoligised and continued driving after I had him pull over for a quiet word. I had never had to explain myself and I certainly was not going to explain myself to a driver.

Benjamin:" what is the problem".

Driver: "there is not one".

Benjamin" come on you do not normally get personal with me".

The conversation went on for a while after answering question that he should not have the answers to Benjamin catches on. The driver knew that he knew and had obviously said somethings that Benjamin had heard before the driver after a long silence can not hold the thought any longer. He puts his foot down shouting as Benjamin hold s on as the driver totally loses his mind

Benjamin at this time is being thrown about the back seats until the driver s thinks that Benjamin is out cold, Benjamin is awake and shouts not with out injuring the driver. The driver's last words were in his last conversation.

Benjamin " what's going on".

Driver " I have told to kill you. I am telling you as a friend".

Benjamin:" I do not believe it have they got you as well". I am a sucker I should have know why now, you do not have to answer me.

The driver says nothing. Benjamin leans over him to remove the keys from the ignition.

The driver continues

Driver:" I was here for that sole purpose."

The driver not knowing his real situation passes out Benjamin checks his pockets of his suit jacket removing his cigarette and lighter. He offers the driver a smoke as he doe's himself he finds little comfort as Benjamin is feeling the same way. Benjamin is finding the whole thing a little bit intense. As his driver takes his last puff of the cigarette and dies in front of him.

Benjamin continues to smoke taking himself away from the death in to a more calmer area in the mind a better mood I suppose he did not the true effects.

Benjamin sits in the car he closes his eyes this time he is traveling forward not backwards as he sits in the car all his memories are flashing back past him. He sees the attempts on his life and he was and the crimes that he was going to have to commit to stay alive. He knows that this was not the end, and he knew that he had trouble coming his way in a very short time. Benjamin was sat in the passenger seat Benjamin believes that he can see the future. Benjamin was not wrong with each of his memories he pieces together the future.

Benjamin catches on just in time his eyes firmly closed as he recovers images after images. As he watches it is like a film, he then sops controlling the thought he rewinds the images watching them in reverse. Only to watch the images sending him back into time when he finally gets total control again he finishes extremely fast in the future he remember everything that he had seen when he finally come s to a stand still. Theirs is silence, but only for a second he opens his eyes trying to understand what had happened. Benjamin can not believe the experience. he is blown away putting slightly he really enjoyed the experience and knew before he started that he would go back he was addicted he had found the ultimate gift. The gift of time travel through the mind.

As he closes his eyes again thinking about what journey that he was going on. He was seeing a lot of the future at that time. Scared of over using his mind of over expression, even so to go to far he stops, there is a knock at his door. He opens his eyes thinking that it was his imagination he ignores the knocking. He opens his eyes and listens for a second time. Suddenly he is looking in to the future and past the a door it was his front door it was broken in. Benjamin was cool and clever as he was expecting this he uses his mind to turn of the lights he thought that was cool, this so called friends from the past had decided to pay Benjamin another visit.

Benjamin knew what was a head of him, as he now had the power to look in to the future he knew for one that there was going to be more than a few of them.

Benjamin knew all there moves he had seen it, suddenly he remembers like a flash back exactly what was going to happen, I will explain. The first guy from the gang forces their way in to Benjamin s home leading the other guys in all of them were armed. As the premonition suggested, Benjamin does not think twice he raises up his arm. He knows that he was going to be the first to open fire. As his first victim come s around the corner and out of his hall way. Benjamin opens fire putting one bullet thought the mans chest. There was more to follow. As Benjamin checks his magazine as Benjamin turns around lucky dodging a few bullets. He takes his next target as a hostage. As he looks for the third as holds his gun towards the mans neck. Benjamin is silent hoping that the man does not call out. Benjamin tells the man not to make a sound. In fact the opposite happened again, Benjamin knew this he had seen the whole thing thought his mind. Benjamin thumps the last of his victims telling him to keep quiet the man who Benjamin had in front of him started to talk as he did he was breaking in to a cold sweat.

Benjamin asks him why he ws sweating, the reply was that if he had a gun to you he would be sweating too.

Benjamin pushes him over on the floor he picks up his gun shoving him in his back. Benjamin speaks to him telling that if he does not want a bullet in the leg Benjamin does not get to finish the conversation as the man stays put with the other man who was put cold into the floor. Benjamin knows that all the trouble that keep on heading his way could be the end of him. As he hold s the man forcing his gun in to his back. Using him as a shield. The last assassin was on his way up to him. The man coming up stairs was making a move. After following Benjamin around his home mean while Benjamin lets the other two go. Benjamin does not go to far as he had closed his eyes to make sure that what he saw had happened. He receives his vision.

Benjamin is getting tough and has to make a decision his first words were who are you as he waits for an answer he gets no reply he gets nothing. Benjamin continues that if you do not show your self to me I will kill your friend here. Benjamin stops thinking about the images that he had seen. Benjamin was on top of the situation he had seen the future. he pushes the man in the back shoving him forwards, Benjamin moves backwards towards the open window with the hostage as he prods the man in the back with his gun, ushing backward s with him. Towards the window with him, his next victim.

Benjamin calls out once more with one dead and another one on it's way. He shouts out you have five minutes to find the question he was counting as he spoke.

Benjamin:" I will give you five minutes to explain if you can not answer you're here is dead".

Benjamin is still counting it was a minute into the time he knew the game the last assassin was thinking how to approach Benjamin as he appears from around a corner of the wall. He waves his arms down Benjamin is happy but he knows exactly what is going to happen as he had seen it. the man puts down his gun correct as he talks to Benjamin correct Benjamin saw that also.

Benjamin could see right through him, he continues to talk, correct brownie point Benjamin was also a wear of that. Benjamin backs up a little bit more as the man try's to talk Benjamin away from the window.

The man:" Benjamin listen it is over you cannot run forever we have men everywhere".

Benjamin :" what you do not do is tell me that it is over it will never be over".

The man:" look Benjamin you are making you self look like a fool why can you not understand that the syndicate is over it is over you have lost, lost".

Benjamin:" No, no you are wrong if I was wrong you would not be standing in front of me, your wrong because if you were right you would not be standing here in front of me".

Benjamin wakes up leaping up off his sofa, knocking his beer of his side table on to the floor he is in shock, he quickly and quietly goes to his front door. As he looks through the small glass window, looking deeply in to the open space, re locking his door. Realizing what had occurred he was imagining and it was not real. He walks to his front room looking and realized that he had left his curtain open he closes them feeling better. It was late as he makes his way back across his living area, and knocks the beer that he was drinking o to the floor again for the second time. He continues to think about what had happened. As he does he falls back into the dream again. He had woken up but still he was dreaming. Everything that had happened to him had happened within the last forty eight hours Benjamin did not know that it ws a dream he was not given the chance to think and way up the pro's and con's before the whole thing started over again.

When Benjamin awakes this time he is in a hospital some where he did not tell me the exact details. All he said was that he had been detained and had to wait for the dream to get out. He told me that it could take days even weeks. His mind was stuck there. if you are wondering who I am I am the writer, I am Benjamin.

Benjamin eventually finds his way back out of his predicament he has left himself on a balcony with one of his men. The man used to work for him Benjamin calls out.

The man :" do not push me".

The man takes another step backwards he is on a ledge the man was willing to jump from the balcony Benjamin thinks that the man will lose his bottle it was extremely high and a log way down. He was pleading to Benjamin not to send him to his death, Benjamin was trying to figure it out he had been told that he was the cause. Even so it was good that Benjamin had no remorse.

Benjamin pushes the man closer to the edge until there is no ledge left the fall slips and falls. Two down one to go. The second man knows that Benjamin means business, and he leaves Benjamin, Benjamin was hoping for that reaction. he did not want another death on his books and there was quite a list. He locks his door, the body that had fallen from his window was left for the police no body said any thing not a word. Benjamin is surprised as it past for suicide as it was the syndicate and nobody messes with the syndicate not even the police.

After pill after pill I was slowly losing my mind, losing my sanity was the hardest thing to come by. Vision after vison. The conversations with people that you would never think. I do not know how it came so personal. I did not ant anybody to take it as I was going insane, or mad even. I was trying to convince myself that I was sane. I was not going anywhere I can a sure you of that.

As I closed my eyes I could see all the kinds of things, it was the waking up that was bothering me as every time I had woken up I would tell myself as I said once in a conversation

" Mental".

This comment was wrong something was not right. The question now was now long will my mind be stable. I did not understand, maybe I did not understand maybe it was true I was mad or maybe I had lost my mind completely.

When I awoke I was in a room it was white I was 0n a bed there was nobody around. I waited, I could feel the large heavy straps forcing my rams down I could have been in a hundred different places and I had to end up here. The question was why me as I gathered my mind I slowly came around thinking that I was in another place a place that was not this one. I was thinking that I was sane or the opposite I was insane and that was the reason that I was their.

After a few weeks of thinking and time does move quickly when you are in the mind. I was not saying to much I got the idea that I was there to help somebody with my lick probably kill them I was on the right lines. The question was who.

94

Although I ws at home, the dream and the visions that I was having seemed to be of the unit I was thinking of god to see if he had any answers to free me from the situation my predicament. I was not in the business of helping people in fact I would feel a lot better if I was just helping my self.

It was not as easy as you may think, I ws saying this to myself as I looked down along the table. I was awake I called out it looked like god was to busy to receive my repentance on un doing the steps that I tired to take.

Chapter ten
Peace keeper

As I stepped down I could at that point help no body although I received enough information on the subject that I was purely there to help not only that I was in my mind trying to d=find the answer to her I was still on the run from my street gangs. As time moved quickly we were talking trough our minds a few minutes seemed like weeks just to get the story correct if I was in the right frame of mind I could have solved it in a week, the mind was a sensitive place a difficult place. As you knew the older you get and if you want to know my age I was thirty it was close to my next birthday not that it made any difference I was still stuck at his moment keeping the peace.

When I awake this time I awake in front of my TV I was a shock as I had not recalled turning it on in the first place. The sound to the programme echoed around my home. as I was still telling my self that it was not real the things that I had dreamt about and the things that I was experiencing. The dreams and things that I had seen in my mind was becoming my mind and the guy that had fallen from the window he worked for me finding out surprise me within the next forty minute s after that thought the police were on my doorstep. They were looking for somebody and had started to question me as if I was the one they were looking for, I ws thinking while being questioned what I had been through was real I kept quiet only to burst out in rage as the dream was not aa dream, it was real. I had to question it why. The question that I to ask myself I came to the conclusion that I had no idea what I was experiencing through my mind I continued well in to the hour I managed to convince the police that I knew nothing and was not involved they were close but not close enough.

As I awoke I was feeling at peace it seemed like all my troubles had become a little far fetched I did not believe it my self but what actually had happened was real. I did not know it at first but everything was real the dreams the traveling the guy that I thought had fallen out of the window which I now no that I pushed him. And the assassin they were real to.

After all of the truth and thinking I was not happy and of course the police now breathing down my neck. However things started to simmer down as I gradually gained control I stopped thinking about the assassins and the killings things were running smoothly again. I was trying to think that what I was experiencing was really real I have to keep on telling my self, just to keep sane. I could not get my head around it every time. I got a certain message something else occurred. I had a little time to think I felt like a murder.

I was seeing this all through the mind I did not know weather it was real or not in fact my life, my mind, did not have the time to work these things out. I ws happy that the problem was moving fast.

I was stupid I was just carrying it as it seemed to be the answer. But it did not look at it as I was being brought back as it was me it was just the way things were. As I closed my eyes I thought that this time I would die. I had already said that more than once. Just reminding myself of the actual danger. While I was there I would be thinking of heaven I did not really care.

Suddenly as I had my eyes closed thinking about the future I bumped straight in to the problem a girl. She was cool and smart and good looking at that point I awoke I was up for a minute thinking about what I just came across I was hoping that she had noticed me I

tired to close my eyes again I ws excited and in a rush. I
was trying to close my eyes again to find her I had no
luck and I was feeling disappointed.

I was thinking about her all day long I was thinking that
I was going to have to make some changes. I wanted
out before somebody killed me. I also wanted to keep
the peace not the kind of peace you may be thinking but
the peace on the streets, there was to much war, to
much killing, to much everything. I was unhappy and I
knew that I had the power. After I had been through my
mind only to be woken up with a cold sweat.
Something had changed it was not the music or the
television, It was me.
Somehow the word was out again that there was a new
kid in town. I closed my eyes, I received what I wanted
I was sending my self back to the beginning, it felt like
I was going along way back to the start of the most
personal thoughts.
At this point the thought like always was blown out of
proportion and was giving Benjamin ideas about
starting a new posy. With his pose down and anew one
arriving. The thought was keeping Benjamin content.
As he lifts a smoke off an old beer can into his mouth it
ws not even a real cigarette it ws one that he had rolled
himself earlier. As he puts in in to his mouth and pulls

on it with his lips the smooth sensation reaches his mind. He was aware for him at that moment that life was a bitch.

I closed my eyes thanking that I was going to change the street, I could not see reality and Benjamin thought of what he wanted most was just a vision.

He could be right knowing that the old posy wanted him dead he had not forgotten about that. And I am not messing around when they say dead they mean dead.

When my mind had calmed down I was ow thinking about peace for some strange reason i will not lie, it seemed that the thought was the ultimate thought as people that in was thinking about also seemed to think the same it was on a level but a dangerous one. It was an dangerous thought. It started a new game within my mind you could never be sure of who you would meet even more so who you would approach you in your mind.

As I closed my eyes the visions were racing in the images that I was receiving were blowing me away, once you were in there was no way out. Until the thoughts had finished if you understand me. I felt good and I felt like I was in a good place if you understand me. nothing had changed I was still in the same place as the last thoughts entered my mind I started another journey and I knew that it was me that had to finish it it was my fault I had nobody to blame.

The word peace had entered my mind it was not a word that you could just pick up and put down it was more complicated than that. I was aware of it. it was something that I had always thought about and having an idea of it left me to believe that it probably wouldn't happen as the thought was embedded in my thoughts stuck in like an knife it was painful it was more painful than trying to put the word down than it was picking it up.

The thought of peace had lead me to believe that I was now screwed, I was scared. That word peace had decided to taken over my mind. As I turned to look at things as much as I liked it seemed to flow to person to person destroying everything as I closed my eyes with the word stuck in me my mind and stuck in my vocal cords. It was like a punch in the face as everybody that I had known and that people would now look at me and laugh I was a laughing stock eventually I understood or at least I thought that I did. I closed my mind and opened up my eyes.

After everything that had happened I had sat down waiting for the next person to enter my mind while I was waiting for the next premonition to take place. I was safe though unhappy, I was having an argument with some guy that I thought was a friend. I was standing at my apartment window I was still trying to figure out weather the vision and all the stuff that I had in mind was real. Weather it was true or false the future was as soft as my furniture. As I laid on the sofa. I was waiting to see the future all I had to do was to sit down. It would not be long before it all begins to happen I could hardly say that I was feeling fine I did not want to close my eyes . and yes there had be a change in my temper I had enough I had wondered to far, to soon, too quickly.

And to top things off I did not understand it still. But it was happening and it was happening to me. I was at peace.

As the weather changed and a storm began, It caught my attention I would normal ignore the weather as it meant nothing to me. I was at my window just picking myself up trying to correct the thought of everything that had happened trying to understand the images that I could clearly see. I came out of my mind I was feeling crazy I had no one to turn to as the feeling did not disperse.

Chapter eleven
The storm

Things were not looking good for Benjamin as he woke
up from a deep sleep straight in to a thunderstorm it
started with a flashing lightening then turning in to a
real proper storm. The lightening hitting the trees in the
background and breaking them down and the annoying
traffic passing by there was a few sound of talking and
people looking for shelter and people being trapped not
being able to find cover. As the storm was getting faster
and bigger . I ws playing it cool I just sat back in my
chair I could see everything from my room.

At the end of the storm I ws still in touch as the small rain drops dripped slowly on to my window ledge. I was thinking who ws thinking about that. I guess it ws one of those things I was so interested with the weather and at that point I had to take some photographs. As I tried to capture what was left it ws a short break from myself and Benjamin.

Benjamin had not approached anybody yet I knew that he was in trouble and I was the person to listen to him, I was the only person who actually trusted him according to him I was not a doctor as such I ws more like a scientist although I was an expert in phycology Benjamin's problems were now our problems. It was a close hit, his problem I believed that had a problem through his mind and I believed that I could help him some how. Maybe he needed some body to talk to.

I asked my self, did not just see a priest his anger was one reason, he was not seeking forgiveness from god. Beside s he said that he would never use a priest he was one. It was not god or forgiveness that he was looking for. he also told me that he w a snot looking for his family something he forgot about when he was younger. I continued as Benjamin was just about to speak. He changes his mind and contuse in silence. We were at his window and Benjamin tells her that they should watch the end of the storm knowing that there was another arriving they should enjoy the storm.

Benjamin had a lot on his mind it ws not going to be one of those fifteen minutes of conversation weather or not he should repent the things that he ws talking about it would takes hours even days and by the state of his mind probably weeks even months as he try's to stop himself giving me the information and details of his crimes. He believed that he committed eventually I was in there he was finally telling the truth. Me and him agreed that it was his mind. He had bowed down knowing that he had lost.

He believed that he was insane but he ws not insane he had something and we wanted it he called it his gift, and he was keeping it to him self. I had to question myself knowing that he could not hide it forever how long he would actually keep it for. before he began to leak all of the secrets within himself the things that he was experiencing comes out.

The question was who would understand him or even more so understand it. who could use it and how long before the public hear about it.

Benjamin refused it was a condition, an illness I thought differently my answers did not make Benjamin feel any better. In fact he left the window space only to come back again. I was concerned as much as him Benjamin was a healed person and I knew him well enough to as I had been watching him to know if he had a problem. As Benjamin was trying to settle pacing around I was following him I was right behind him he did not turn around Benjamin stopped and I stepped in front of him as I was close enough to kiss him I waved my had up had them down his face he had no idea that I was there the girl steps a side quickly as Benjamin returns again to the window. I called out to him quietly he could not hear me at first I call him again getting a little bit closer. He had ignored me for the third time I let him go.

Benjamin knows that his problems are his own and the mind had many places and what dwelt there in his mind was his own doings he had know one to blame. Although not being put off by his own experiences with his own mind knew that he would find away back he was not thinking about himself which made a change for him as he was naturel, greedy. He waited for his own life to back his own life which was Benjamin. The drugs, the fights, and the women, and the partying as much as god he believed that he would control his own status eventually by himself. He was trying to put the fact of what he had experienced aside he could not believe it but we knew different.
He was not thinking and was thinking that there ws some other way and started looking for different

solutions. He was feeling and thinking that way because I was there.

He had not forgotten about his previous experienced and I a=that was something that I was banking on. With the gangs and posies out of the way he made a statement to a priest that he had finished and promised that would get everything that he lost back, hard words I thought.

If it meant the death of him he preyed extremely long still telling himself that he would win again that was me forcing his ego.

Benjamin ws now thinking straight extremely as he leave s the church as he walks past the priest at the door he was walking outside and not thinking that he had got anything out of it and it seemed a waist of time thinking of what he had just said. The ground that Benjamin was walking on ws wet and the sky that was above had darkened he realized exactly how long he kept the priest there. he covers his face with his scarf as he walks in to the moon light as it hits his face. he records the time in the distance there is another storm brewing. He makes his way through town watching everything, watching his dark shadow, he stops as he sees something he thinks at first it ws a girl, he looks again and still nothing he closes his eyes this time it felt force full like there was something blocking his mind that part was real.

As Benjamin closes his eyes he is talking through his mind he is standing by the window not noticing looking downwards right at one of his posy. The man below had a gun it was pointing right at Benjamin. This time it was not a vision it was real. Benjamin was hard enough to just stand there but instead he goes outside to greet the man the man believes that he had lost his target in fact it was now right behind him. Benjamin clutches the man, the man pleads with Benjamin, Benjamin was not down there to play games. He pulls the man closer pointing the mans gun at the man after taking it from him unloads all the bullets on to the floor except for one. He knew the man a he was from Benjamin gang. Benjamin tells the man to stay put the man does not listen he take another step backwards as if he was going to make a break for it. Benjamin has to think fast was he going to kill him.

Benjamin awakes in a cold sweat he is on his sofa he notices that his window is open he does not close the window at first he takes a good look around his apartment he walks to his front door it is open. This quizzes Benjamin he then walks to the window and doors which were open then closes them Benjamin is confused and lays back on his sofa.

It was late when Benjamin gets a call from a old friend
this does not normally happen., he was confused and
after it upset the girl in question needed a hundred
grand even though I had the money I was a little
reluctant to give it to her. I closed my eyes again which
as you can see has become a little habit as I closed my
eyes as I did this time it seemed to me that I was always
trying to hide from the actual problem by closing my
eyes it seemed to me be the way in to the future away
of running I could hardly say no for the state of my
position, I told the girl to come over to my place. She
agreed and we made the date and a time.
As I wondered off totally forgetting for that moment
and her call I was still stuck in my mind it could not of
come at a better time as he was coming in at the same
time as my assassin, I could see everything through my
mind things were getting clearer. The only thing that I
did not have was total control and control was time. As
the visions came and went especially from the past I
could see everything before and after too. They did not
know that I welded this gift somebody was protecting
me I thanked him for that.

CHAPTER

FORTEEN

GRIND

After all the excitement of the last couple of days I was coming to the terms that I was going to be killed or kill. As I laid down on my sofa the only place that I would go. I was thinking about what I had actually experience still finding no answers to what it was called the last few days. I suppose you could call it a week or so I was now interested of how the mind worked. I was no doctor and I did not want to visit one as in the modern world saying the things that I have experienced but with no answers would not help my situation if explained by me. saying the things that I experienced talking about them could get me locked up. As time went by I was still focused although my life to me seemed to me to be full of the not worthy. As I sat back down I was just staring in to the front room I was looking for something to focus on. I needed help I had nobody to turn to I was asking myself the question was I going mad.

I was thinking the worst what if the word got out, and how many people in my own street gang would turn away loyalty is hard to find. I mean surprisingly and seriously I could not imagine being taken for a mental guy, it does not look to good on your CV. That is curriculum vitae. I wanted to close my eyes I knew that it was a good journey into a safe place I knew this world again I was thinking at this point who else does this. What kind of a person and what kind of behaviour was this and what a would finally happen if I stayed in there to long. As I sat and answered all the questions that I was putting to you, all I had experienced in the last week I was coming to the conclusion that it was true I had become a made person I could not tell anybody I kept it to myself I had visitors again just friend and closer friends.

But again as soon as they walked in they walked out, after I had discussed my problems with them it ws not long before the people on the street knew I did not want to say it to people I was ashamed and I was made to feel it, I did not want people to say my name it was now Crazy Benjamin. It hurt at first as a joke and wore off quicker than I had thought. I knew that in was not mad. I think I just picked the wrong friends for now. At one point there was a group of men standing outside my home I was looking the other way when a melon few straight past me landing at my front door when I looked around they had gone it was to late to manhandle them I could hardly contact the police.

I knew that people were talking differently, I pushed my key in to my door opening the door softly pushing it open how I got into the building with out being hurt by the crowed area down stairs I do not know but I did. I did not care I was content in putting the banter aside my home ws cool I could finally relax.
As I was sitting down rolling a cigarette a I pushed it into my mouth lighting it as I took a few puffs at that time still in the same place. I closed my eyes hoping to see some thing anything that would take my mind of the last few days events. As I lived in a large space even though I thought that the space was never big enough, and I always wanted more. Simply for the fact that I needed the space to party. I would get high on beer and walk around the doors. Looking at pictures and things of the past, I could never get out of my mind of how wealthy I actually was. And that was the thought that was keeping me together. And tat was the thought that was keeping me happy.

As I moved around from door to door I was falling in love with the place again. That's when I awoke I ws surprised it was only a dream I sat up quickly thinking how good that was I wanted to go back there it ws so peaceful I knew that I would never see the place again.

I wanted that dream to reoccur I thought about it over and over I wanted to venture in to it seemed a good way of escaping but it was also addictive. Thinking about the other journeys that I had taken through my mind this one was the best.

I was trying to find out how dreams worked and I read in a magazine some where just recently. They could be reoccurring when I read this a big smile came up upon my face I was lost at that point of what to think. But I was also happy to read this. If it ws true I was going ion an adventure. This also meant that I had a meaning or some kind of meaning. Again I was happy to read of this. On this occasion the dream that I wanted did not occur the dream that I did not want occurred I was standing up at the time I ws standing on top of a roof just above the top floor, for some reason it had reached my conscious I was telling my self to move I was approached by a stranger I had not seen him before he did not tell me his name after I had met that man few things had changed in my mind. It was important and frustrating. Thinking to think about it I was stuck and could not figure it out if it was real or if I had made It up. or it had already happened I had seen the future, all I know is that man had hit the floor a few minutes later. After the shock of this experience I was looking at visions and dreams a little more seriously it was that dream that persuaded me to go up to the top of the building on to the roof. Where I saw the man in first place. I waited for him to appear as there ws a cold breeze of the wind blowing I could see across the whole town I was right I had a visitor it ws weird as I was thinking about that man as he slowly appeared to me again he walked as I remembered his feet making a ghostly sound as if his shoes were to big for him. His dark hair long and tied back. He had a gloomy look on his face a worn out look from a distance. He ws one that you you would not approach if you saw him walking down the street, at this point I wanted to open my eyes, already knowing the man's future. he did not notice me, he was not being there.

I was not sure if it had happened or if it was going to happen I could see his sorrow from where I was standing that cold stare on his face as he walked past me with out saying a word. I opened my eyes not before travelling in to his mind just to find out the real and true answers of why he was there after I had taken a good look around. After this I brought myself back into my mind I was seeing everything that was going to happen well in to the future the first message was not to approach him tat ws to bad I had already done this. The second was tat he with me was going to jump off the building as the man was completely insane. Before I had a chance to talk to him he was on the ledge. The man on the ledge this looked straight at me that's when he knew that's when I noticed him, I knew him I could not remember his name but he was one of my very old gang the white dragons, as I rushed to wards him as he jumped he shouted that they had got everybody and I was next the mans last words were that as he was about to jump he stumbles as I quickly moved to wards him as he slips not going over the edge he ws holding on with both arms realizing what he was doing that was bad luck before I got there his arms gave way as he left I just managed to grab him I was not strong enough to pull him back in to safety he fell to his death. As he fell he yelled out my name Benjamin that was my name the rest knew who I was as I knew who they were.

Why he let go of the ledge I did not know all I do know that there was a message in there somewhere for me. something to do with the future. I legged it down stairs twenty flights and then outside bumping straight in to a police. And a medical assistant as I bumped in to them they were looking at the mess on the concrete floor. As I pushed the assistant out of the way yelling at him that I knew that guy. I had made a mistake as I just lost the will to speak even as they all looked at me as if I was the one that did it. I tried to explain I was not waiting around to be questioned I knew straight way that I was a suspect I was not going to wait to be questioned or arrested. that is when I ran as I pushed the assistant out of the way and made a run for it. I knew that they thought that I had pushed him they came down the stairs quickly I bet they did not even have a look at the scene. I raised a few questions for running off this action did not make anything any easier I knew the law I knew they were on to me. I needed to make a few quick decisions to heal a few demons. The first I would give myself up as I had done nothing but watch and go with them accordingly or go for a long run, I needed to see the future.

I turned up back at the crime seen I was taken in to custody extremely quickly I told them that I had no were to hide and I was not the man they were looking for I told it as it was that the man jumped I tried to grab him but failed and he fell. I did not want to go down town to the police station and I was not in the mood this evening to plea insanity, I was on my own this time no body to bail me out. None of the boys were there to back me this time if the police get it wrong I will be doing time. I ws thinking fast I wanted to make a run for it again yes I was that scared of them. even though the man on the floor was an old friend I kept that quiet for now it was bound to come out when they questioned me I think I explained that to them I could not recollect due to the shock of the whole thing it good that I had actually had forgotten his name. I kept telling myself that I was not doing time for something I did not do and especially not for that scum bag.

I had been cuffed after I had written my account of things I decided to stick to my end of the story I told the truth to the police, it was there move.

Before I had the chance to explain they were saying amongst themselves that I had thrown the man off the building off the roof off the roof of the apartment block

I had no choice I was holding back they new that already I was not prepared to tell them that I was having visions when they came to question my health I told them as good as yours. The truth was at the time I was having visions of death I knew that did not sound to good. I knew in ws called to the roof to help him in fact the opposite had happened. For the next day or two I was in a cell. Cold tea, cold coffee, and toast which did not look like toast. They finally let me go. After they realized that I was innocent. When I finally got out side I could feel the freedom it was only two days it felt like a hundred. I was in a different town that was typical now all I had to do was find my way home. I had not realized that I had been driven out of town a totally new place, this is wear things get hard, I was wales but I came from London or there about it was not going to be an easy way home there ws obviously going to be some trouble and it ws obvious to me that the police were behind the next part of this adventure.

I could smell it I could see more than they could see more than they could imagine. It was the police they were setting the whole thing up. as soon as I stepped out side of there building I knew that I was taking a chance with my life. I was looking for directions to the train station it was going to take the train home I must of past out somewhere on the journey as I have no recollection or no memories of getting on to the train instead I found myself on a coach. As I got off the coach as I walked through the town I ws looking at the signs some were in English I was wise to follow the word s written in English keeping a very low profile I was walking in the right direction at least I was not right out in the country side I could have been in places and thanked the thing that knocked me out I did not

117

wait to ask the coach driver who put on the coach in the first place. I was just happy to be there. as I stuck to the street I was guiding myself I could not just ask anybody for help as I would have been given the wrong directions. I suppose that you could look at it as a cheap frill if you like that sort of thing. I was keeping my head down as I was looking for the train station and I was right I was going in the wrong direction due to asking some bloke for directions I finally got the journey that I was trying to make correct I went back to the right way by following the sign posts I found it within fifth teen minutes. As I mad my way within the fifteen minutes that I was walking the town erupted there were people ,cars ,buses. I could forget about keeping a low profile I actually felt I ws being followed I was in danger. I did not like it I had no body to watch my back I had to do that myself. This was not easy but was do able.

My head was down I focused on the concrete path ignoring all the traffic around me all it wold take was one person to take a dis likening to me about anything the way I walked, the way I spoke and the clothes that I was wearing all played it's part. I knew that some one up there was guiding me with luck, and with that I found the train station.

As I got to the train station with luck and it was even lucky that it fell on the day that the ticket guards day off he was not there. I took advantage of this I was traveling for free. I walked through the gate, I was on my way home. it would take me most of the day, I cannot remember how I managed to pass out and end up the way did. And how I got to the town and did not know, as I walked down the platform as the train approached I was feeling hungry I went of to find some food there was always some body's left over food lying on the luggage rack if I was really lucky I might even find some food that had not been touched I was right again within a few minute I had found some as I reached up and pulled a small box of the shelf I was delighted with what I had found. It was a box of chocolates probably left by mistake and forgotten a present that would now never get to the real owner. I felt kind of guilty especially If it was a gift to a loved one I thought at least it went to somebody who needed it. After that I went off to look for some more knowing that there was half a chance that I would find something again this time it was a box of grapes, I thought as I tucked in. This time trying not to think of the real owner,

I was happy that they had been left and I thanked god again for his generosity. I had checked the whole train and there was nothing else. I think two gifts from the strangers was enough,

That is when I awoke again this time in a cold sweat and all disoriented not knowing where I was but in fact I was at home nice and safe. Only for the thought, I was grinding my self I was believing that I was the cause of everything that had happened I knew this I was grinded.

Chapter fifteen
RE-SET

When I re-set my mind and got on top of the visions
that I was having that I could see I had finally found the
gift. In my mind this gift was the second gift, as I
looked forwards and not backwards I had the gift to see
the future. I had to ask my self if it was real or not, was
it a real gift or not or was it that I had just bumped into
something that a crazy person would talk about, I was
left thinking.
I needed to get away I was thinking away, some where
out of the country as such so I booked my self a plane
ticket to the united states of America. I had to re-set my
mind.
All was well I made the visit, the London airports, they
seemed extremely busy. I was hoping that on body
would noticed me. As I got there by taxi as I got out of
the taxi the driver was not particularly polite as I gave
him the fare and he took it out of my hand and drove
off quickly he beeped, leaving me at the entrance, as I
walked in to the airport it was like a totally different

world. I was at the start of an extremely exciting journey. I was making a journey that could change the rest of my life, it was a way of escaping the drugs and the crime, I was putting the rest of it way behind myself.

That was the my last thought, as I was awoken up by the sound of my door bell I found myself laying half on and half off my sofa, the whole thing was a dream. I had not gone anywhere I was still at home. some how as I awoke I looked around I was disappointed that it was only a dream and I was just dreaming, I went to my front door to answer it.

I had a question to put to the dreams that I was having I had to ask myself and I did was why I was dreaming again I woke up I was dreaming everything that I was thinking of was a dream after all the fun in the end the dream was disappointing as I wanted it to continue. I woke up and stood next to the sofa which I was laying on only to fall back upon it. I was disappointed that it was a dream and was not real. I was telling myself to get used to it as I had a feeling that this was going to be on going.

Within the next few months these dreams and visions continued constantly they had quickly taken over my life day in and day out the constant thinking of trying to understand them. the watching it was enough to send anybody including myself insane. It became a habit it was the adrenaline it was addictive like alcohol and had a power like smoking or any other drug that I had taken and there was a few.

I had sat down for the first time in the last several hours, I was tired I had been many places through my mind helping people, and then the total opposite people destroying people.

It ws now my time I was doing this not for friends or people that I had working for me or even people that I had worked for. it was for me, perfect I closed my eyes once more I was not looking for the future this time I was going back into the past to meet with myself. It was a simply normal journey but I new that it was going to have some effects in the future.

As I moved around the room in my mind there I was in a party it looked to me if I was watching some of my old memories. as I caught on I it was getting emotional I had began to cry. It was like me to cry when things I see make or hear.

I did not want to be where I was I closed my eyes after I had seen the images of myself I wanted to come back I wanted to come home.

This time I had to put up with real fights it was like I was bring the images back with me they had clung on to me. I panicked, as the things in my living room were getting more out of control out of hand. Lucky within that second as I thought my mind changed reversing everything I was now moving forward where I wanted to be it was like watching a film in fast forwards until it stopped. As I re-set my mind for the second time this time I was moving into the future. how far in to the future I could not tell you but I was there. as I got there was more calming feeling and I was a little more confident. I was looking down upon myself again. I had not clothes on the first thing I needed to do was to find them. I was at the party the same party as I had just visited except I was in the future so as I gathered exactly what information that I needed to bring myself back it seemed to me that I was at the same party meeting the same people but in the future. if that makes sense I had to travel back to be able to travel forwards in time only to find myself in the same place in the future. weird I know.

For some strange reason the people in the room were staring at me, that was because I had no clothes on. Lucy a girl who was not to shy approached me she moved extremely close to me as I closed my eyes believing that she w as going to make a pass presses a button on my arm which I had not noticed before as she let go the clothes appeared on my body. I looked down at them know believing that I had perceived myself

well into the future. some how I managed to find
myself mixing with high society.
As I moved away I called to her she turned around
knowing exactly what I was going to say.
I hesitated.
Benjamin:" what is your name".
The girl:" Lucy my name is Lucy".
Lucy continued to walk off.
Benjamin:" Thank you". Benjamin calls out to her.
She ignored Benjamin's last compliment Benjamin was
just making conversation.

Lucy thinks that Benjamin was trying to ask her out
after she had approached him as she helped him.
Benjamin stands on his own as other guest talk about
the way he is dressed Before he had met Lucy. For the
second time in that one evening he was saved again
and again it was Lucy pulls Benjamin aside this time
she starts an argument telling him to buckle up as there
was many important people in the room he was
embarrassing them. at that point as Lucy try's to pull on
his arm he awakes as he manages to take and control
his mind back to it's original place in him. As he find s
his way back he was getting a better knowledge of how
his new gift works. The gift that he was experimenting
with. Image after image Benjamin wants back in he was

keeping this gift quiet he did not want to share it as much as he did not want to speak about it was good that he could keep his mouth shut. It was personal Benjamin falls asleep again on his sofa now that he had made his way back. He could easily get three people on it. as the night goes on Benjamin is tossing and turning in his sleep he ends up the other way around in his bed as he shifts occasionally in the night.

As the early morning comes around Benjamin awakes he is feeling rough as he tries as he tries to find himself he falls and basically straight on to his floor he questions why he had fallen. As Benjamin picks himself up off the floor it happens again. As he hits the edge of the sofa on his way down stopping the full impact of his fall. Eventually he forces himself back half up on his knees he picks himself up off the floor it was ten times harder than his hang over which was just about to kick in.

Benjamin knows he has got trouble coming he could see it miles off it was on the cards. Not that he was really bothered. He had been through everything else. A little arguing would set him up to wake from the gift. He had already seen the outcome except he did not know the strength of what was about to occur with the actually thought doing the damage.

Three days later Benjamin is standing on his balcony as he watches the sun rest in the sky. As he watches with ease, as he watches the sky it turns from light blue, blue and then orange like state then just as it goes down it tuned the calm evening in to total darkness. Benjamin is happy as he awaits for the moon which was out just the other side of the sky.

Again Benjamin is happy, but not out of control he did not let it go to his head. Like most people would as he turns away keeping the thought of what he saw to himself telling himself that it is another day tomorrow. Benjamin knows that if he closes his eyes almost scared as a child would lay in the darkness clinging to his bedding. The darkness had no body to turn to. The position that he was in reminded him of being a child for the next few days he has a few dreams his dreams at this point were about everything.

As Benjamin fights for control of his mind and consciousness while taking a little journey through his mind he was hoping that it would stop and come to an end. How wrong his visions were things seemed to be working in reverse. Benjamin needed a change of scene And within a few minutes he had made up his mind he packs up some clothes and leaves.

As he packs his bags one by one it was like it was out of control he grabs his essentials clothes, passport, driving licence, he checks his wallet over and over making sure that it is all there and looks deeply in to his mind. There was something playing on Benjamin's mind.

He knew and did not attempt to understand it at that time.

Benjamin heading out of town for the second time Benjamin was confused as he had lost all sense of everything accountable to his behaviour

Benjamin steps out side believing that it would be safe it was far from his idea. He leaves his apartment and walks to the car park about two hundred yards, There was no traffic at this time he looks at his watch it was about one thirty in the afternoon by half two he had got in to his car. Benjamin was about to met his maker.

Benjamin can feel that something is wrong as Benjamin walks to his car a car drives past, lights on shinning them straight I to Benjamin eyes, Benjamin raises one arm partially blocking the light by covering his face. thinking that it was just another person. Benjamin chooses to ignore it as Benjamin thinks it is just another person setting off on there journey but in fact it was something different. Benjamin still walking thinking about his discovery as he walks to his car readying him self to take his car out for a ride out of touch Benjamin doe's not see a car races towards him hitting Benjamin throwing up and over on to the bonnet Benjamin hits bonnet hard then the ground harder.as he tries to pick himself up of the concrete floor the car had turned around and was on it's way back. Benjamin picks himself up, waiting.

Benjamin does not stand a chance as the car hits him again. Benjamin lays still in the road on the ground not being able to move the car with it's passengers drive away.

When Benjamin awakes he finds himself on a stretcher as he finds himself not in the place which was supposed to be in his car he lays on the white bed covered with white sheets as he fights to breathe falling in and out of his consciousness he is in working order his mind is damaged and he is awaiting surgery. As he is already in his mind in a mind. You would have to experience it yourself to actually understand it. knowing sub consciously that he w as being taken cared of he tries to open his eyes as he does he can see lights in front of his face as he looks up at the celling he can see even more. Hoping that he was not dying and was not going to go upwards. As he insists that he is dead. In a second when he finally pulls through he could hear two maybe three people discussing weather he should die or live.

As they continued to talk to Benjamin it was true he was finally coming around as he wakes forcing him self upright only to fall back down. Benjamin knows that he has made it he knew that he was alive.

As Benjamin awoke he was paused up right sitting on his bed the last thing that he wanted to do was to start thinking of old demons he was not impressed. He was thinking of old school friends thinking and fighting not to let them in to his mind. As he was trying to find away out. Benjamin looking at things of the past and of the future was going to continue for a while. In conversation old school mates kept on popping up. Benjamin did not like it but he was clever enough to continue excepting it Benjamin closes his eyes again.

CHAPTER

SIXTEEN

HANG OVER

I was busy at the bar getting drunk, it was the end of the day, I was hung over from the night before. No it is no butts I was seriously drunk and getting out of my mind. As I sat there keeping myself to my self I was feeling quite easy in fact somehow I managed to buy the whole bar a drink. In the morning I was sent the bill it came to around a thousand pounds. Either way in the morning I would walk out still drunk. I was hung over. I was feeling seriously ill. I had drunk to much, I was leaving the bar. I was sick everywhere on three occasions I thought that I was going to die. I agreed from that point that beer was not the answer. It was not the answer to the solution.as I fell asleep on the a bench on the street I was waiting answers from god. I was realizing that the only god was going to be me. I tried so hard to believe in what I was seeing.

As I was sick again and fell over some guys fence then in to a bush, then hedge I closed my eyes thinking that I did not want to be here. As I was on my back I looked upwards towards the sky the night time clouds had hustled them sleeves above me it was time to go home. in saying that I did not want to go home it was a first for me that I was going to spend the rest of the night on the street. Only for the fact that I did not know where I was. Not only that I was to far from home to make it back there.

I woke up after falling asleep again in another bush next to me a tree fifty yards away a shop as I thought about approaching it I guess what you guessed some more booze.

I got off the lightly wet ground from the dew was on the grass it was nearly winter as I picked up my self up off the ground, I was heading for the shop, for some booze.

I had achieved the situation of being in a shop that had closed five hours ago, as I picked up the package of beer I was lucky that I had got in there not to wake up the neighbours or the owner who was probably asleep up stairs or staying up there scared and waiting for me to leave. I had walked in there to find a fix.

Within a few minutes I had found myself again robbing the shop brought back a lot of memory's again I was on my way. I poured the drink straight down my mouth, I was thinking at that time it was good and somethings never change, gladly it would not be me. after steeling a rather large amount of alcohol I went back to the bushes

with the tree that would be the place that I was staying
the night as it would be to dangerous to walk home I
would wait until the morning. I could not believe that I
was hoboing due to the fact that I had a luxury home
waiting for me. mind you I needed a change of the
scene   and this looks like this was it.

As I dropped my hand down on to my leg while sitting
down trying to move into a normal more suitable more
comfortable position. I was thinking about the whole
experience through my mind. I had to be careful I was
finding out that the mind moves just as fast even faster
than your mouth or the other away around. I found that
thought was my problem.

What I believe that was happening was that I was hung
over. I had done it again I had too much to drink, Well
to much beer.

I was trying extremely hard to throw up and sober
myself up, it was not as hard as I thought eventually the
fluid came out, but it was not with out pain only to find
myself back to the beginning, I was back on my sofa
then on top of the building everything that had
happened everything that I had seen as for the
misguidance and mistakes I was stuck I could not
believe it. I thought that it was all real but in fact it was
not it was just my imagination playing games with me
playing games with my mind and myself this time it
was real within a few minutes I was coming back down
to earth, there was a knock on my door, I tried my
hardest not to answer it. but the knocking was
continuous.

I was not the type to bottle out, and this person
knocking on my door was not the end of my torments, it
was bound to happen again. As much as I wished to
ignore it. and as lonely as I was I had to answer, it was
funny as soon as you get out you are dragged back in
the same old bullshit. They say that life s a circle this
one was. I was fighting for my own life at this point
although it did not bother me at this time to much. I was
upset because there was two guys on my door step. All
in all somebody at the top was pissed off. He ws
thi9nking of me so he has sent a couple of his boys to
me I wished I could just send them back although it is
not like I have not been roughed up before.
As I remember it started off just the two of them in the
end I told them to go home I was lucky that they were
in a good mood and it was just a conversation on there
behalf.
It seemed to me that I was still paying my dues I
managed to keep it on a level the worst thought as we
were talking was I hope that they were not armed in

saying that I had a whisky bottle right next to me with my base ball bat by my door just in case things got a bit rough.

After there visit I was feeling like a watched man a feeling that I had not felt for a long time.

As I closed my door after wishing them good day I went and sat down on my sofa putting the whisky bottle down and picking up my gun it was loaded and ready to use just in case they came back.

As I woke I could see everything clearly right from the start as it started I was in my mind I could see it so clearly at first there was a busy street and a couple of stretched limos turned up both white it could not have been any clearer. The next thing I saw was eight assassins step[ping out of the crowed pavilion the street came to a stand still I was in my mind watching carefully as all eight of the men approached the building I checked my magazine the first four took the lift the second four took the stairs I knew that it was going to be a close call. I had to make a decision to stay put or find another way out. Which was in hand at that moment I climbed out of the window I did not want to go down as it looked near enough impossible as going up was even though it was only two floor up on the top of the building.

I decided to wait it would only be a few minutes and they would have reached the top I braced myself closing my eyes I could see everything within my own future of what was going to happen to me again there's a knock at the door the first four of eight of the assassins had arrived I could not believe it that they had made it to my door they even knew the door number. The question was I going to answer it. the answer to that I guess it would be me. I continued.

Benjamin:" Arhh can I help you".

After I had spoken to them giving myself away, I moved quickly ducking the cannon fodder as they approached as they did I hit the floor avoiding the hail of bullets and returning fire. As they all now knew that I was at home.

As my first victim of four hit the deck I was not sure if I had got him that was after they had blown my front door off. I found him quickly dragging further from his team I was going to use him as a way of escaping and put a couple of bullets in his leg just to make sure that he stayed with me. he fell faster than fly's the second guy falls to the floor my aim was good today I picked him off the floor and shot him in the legs throwing him in the same place as his friend after removing his weapons. A hail of bullets destroying the hall way walls.

As all this was the beginning I had kind of played back the images that were in front of me not the images that were in front of me I had lost control of my future changing the future and ended up some how back in the past while being in the future I bean by not know it was like my old self some how. I was pulled all the way back into the blast but only for a second as I was pulled through the carnage leaving all what I had seen in the past back in to the future as the third hitman attempted me I had no knowledge of the four assassins on the stairs, I plucked the third in my living room leaving one more, by firing a couple of rounds in to them they were all dead. I needed space to move into and at this moment I could feel their presents on the stairs even though I was forty metres away. I did not know at that point I had more company as there ws people rushing out of there homes screaming and shouting.

As I slowly stood at my front door just peaking around the door edge, as I made it too the fire exit door I could hear the footsteps they were getting nearer they were coming for me.

Eventually the footsteps came to a halt Benjamin stops, as he points his gun around the cold half lit stairs listening for any sound at first there is nothing there was silence he was listening really hard while down stairs just close he hears something drop it was a gun magazine it hits the floor making a small sound which=h echoed upwards they were there Benjamin knows that they know his position he waits just for that moment as he looks around him and over his shoulder that something was the shadow of his suit sleeve of a jacket that was enough Benjamin is back in business he knows that they are there.

He moves quickly down the stairs looking around and focused as the footsteps stop he has found the fifth assassin pointing his gun at the man Benjamin pulls the trigger leaving the dead on the floor he is dead not wounded Benjamin kicks the assassins gun aside and makes sure that he is dead as he does the sixth assassin appears opening fire as he does Benjamin again picks up the body of the dead assassin hiding behind it as it takes in more gun fire only to be thrown at the sixth man giving Benjamin a chance to return gun fire as the dead body falls off the man Benjamin gets lucky and makes a wound that leave the man dead he shot him in the chest. The next assassin is in the position of being killed he bumps straight into Benjamin as Benjamin was checking the sixth assassin for clips and guns.

Benjamin looks upwards knowing that he has his gun on him as he raises his arm only thinking of one thing thinking that he would have to be quick for this draw. If he was quick enough for the draw, Benjamin gets the message on this occasion Benjamin not quick enough although he has a bit of luck the assassin fire s first a couple of rounds Benjamin awakes it was just a dream, as Benjamin awakes he is sitting up right on his sofa he walks to his bedroom being in bed would be more comfortable and more dangerous in Benjamin position.

As he runs his hands through his hair and then over his body just to check himself over he was thankful that it was only a dream.

As he picks himself, he finds his gun he was thinking at the time was a dark one for him. And the days were getting darker. Benjamin rises of his bed he walks to his kitchen and makes himself a drink of coffee as he could not be bothered to wait for the kettle to boil he finds himself a cold beer out of his fridge leaving the kettle on to resolve it's self.

The fridge was a cold and dark place he looks at the food in the fridge it was a gone off take away.

As Benjamin looks at the food he is tempted to indulge there was nothing left in his kitchen cupboard only Chinese gone off rice and half eaten noddle, Benjamin at this point did not care a meal is a meal and when you have nothing I guess you would make of what you have it was not like Benjamin to a saint he could of easily ordered somethings he realized that he was not the only person starving at this moment. As he lifts the tub of noodle out of the fridge he turns quickly grabbing the folk simultaneously and makes his way in to the gone off food.

He closes his eyes as he claws in to the dish another mouthful, and then another as he ids telling himself that it tastes ok knowing in fact that it tasted disgusting. It was all or nothing Benjamin says to himself as he starts to eat the rice he puts his hand into the fridge pulling out a beer a brown bottle with a screw lid. The only thing that was missing was a pickled onion Benjamin was thankful not for the fact that there was one but the fact that there was not one. Benjamin walks away he had punished himself enough. Why was the question when he was just looking for some normality

As Benjamin slowly finishes the last mouthful of the rice he is back in control maybe the decision to eat the rice ws the right decision he closes his eyes not expecting as he is back watching his old friends his old posy and they are now waiting to make an attempt on his life. Benjamin is out and about he had gone to do some shopping in town he did not venture there to often the reason was that he was known by too many people. He did not think that he had the bottle te guts to do it. As he walks through the shopping centre at first there was nobody but it seemed to Benjamin as he recalls one minute there was nobody and the next it was filled with people he did not know even people that he did no he did not know. It was like he was being protected somehow Benjamin was in gods eyes this happened on three occasions. As time went by he had forgotten about the street until the day that he was walking home through a smaller part of the town it was quiet although it was all in the mind But it did not feel like it.

As it seemed I was sitting in town at the sandwich bar I had already ordered some food as I lifted my cup up I was fine at that moment I then stood up taking the tray that my food was on off the tray and placing the food down on the table it looked to me that I was no longer in the town in fact I was in town only I was in an

American town. As I sat down not to make my true feeling out I continued to drink my coffee. As I was just about to start eating I had a vision I stopped eating straight away spitting the pie and cream out turning a few heads the waiter rushed over asking me if I was all right only to force me to knock over my coffee as I stood up she thought that I may be choking only for my coughing as both the pie and the coffee e had gone down the wrong way as she grabbed me in a position I a=cannot remember its real name some kind of life saving hug from the behind. Eventually I managed to get her off as I calmed her down instead of myself. It was too late to open my eyes and I wanted to keep them closed as I knew that it was not real it was only a vision or a day dream or even a dream but this time it was different the people gathered around me but they were not the people that I had expected if any. I bumped straight into a street gang who happened to entertain my pie before I had a chance to calm down I believed that I was in a America I had been there before it was a totally different experience I did not know exactly what I said or what in had done maybe the gang were just looking for trouble.

I could see it coming a mile off I was trying to wake but I was getting nowhere as the gang had turned around they were not just satisfied with my pie they now wanted me. as the gang of youths approached him.as they had knocked the food that Benjamin had ordered on to the floor off the table, preparing them selves and getting in the mood as I tried to tell them that I had no arguments with them the gang refused to leave and my interfering mouth was not helping my situation. I was hard and it looked like I was going to have to pick a fight as most of the customers had dispersed I was left

on my own. As I went to stand up I was pushed back down as they circled around me. I had a choice I chose to make a move. I had already had my hands clenched as the first man approached me as he pushed me I grabbed his hand and broke it after I pushed him face down through the table stupidly I let him go the second man stepped forwards he was nothing I did him with a punch to his chest some how they had got behind me grabbing me from behind I managed to wriggle out of his hold, using a push to put him on to the floor.
In the end I had fended them off only to cause more trouble as I had blew my cover by leaving three out of the four guys on the floor. My excuse was that I ws had to protect myself I was legal, they were not.
Why I was legal because in my heart I still owned the streets I was legal because I had a licence to protect myself, They did not. As I walked away that is when I heard the click as I turned around that is when I knew what was going to happen one of the men picked himself off the floor he had a gun.
Benjamin:" it looks like I did not hit you hard enough".
I raised my hand s I was shot and just on e more thing it was more than once. I thought I was dead, while I was traveling back through my mind the weird thing about it even when I had awoke the wound was there as I awoke in shock with everything had happened I had brought a wound back from a dream something that I always thought was not real I had brought something from the future in to the past. I was sitting on my sofa. As I fell on to the floor the blood was dripping out of me I had an idea of what to do. As I walked to my kitchen to find a bandage to tidy myself up I was scared to close my eyes I was worried that I would take myself back there as I fixed my wound I noticed that the wound was as bad as I thought.

With blood pouring out of me I tried to bandage my self
it was working in a sense at that point Daniel the dog
turned up knocking on my door I knew it was him but I
had no idea what he wanted yet. I scrambled out of my
kitchen to my front door as I looked through the spy
glass it was him. I knew this not only by seeing him but
I could see that he was holding is arm. He was here to
assassinate me I quickly raised my arm as I was armed
too, I was not speaking or answering the door and it
was like Daniel to force his way in just for the simple
fact to show that somebody had been there. I was
standing up nice and quiet he makes an approach.
Daniel the dog:" hay Benjamin are you there".
Benjamin did not answer and knew not to answer him
as Benjamin looked through the spy hole one of the two
Luke brothers turned up also as that point I hit the deck
as an array of bullets hit the door way as I dived on to
the floor only to get up and leg to the nearest place of
cover which was the end of the hall way. I was forced
even further back until I had nowhere else to hide I was
now on my window ledge it was a long way down
there. I had no choice but to try and climb up in stead of
down.

At first I was just standing there then I was hanging
there they had entered the apartment I was hanging
about four feet off my balcony ledge. As soon as they
thought that I was not a home I climbed back up wards
as I climbed up wards I could hear them smashing the

apartment up. I climbed further all I could think was not to look down. I did not know weather I had reached the top all I knew at that time I was on the fourteenth floor as I climbed upwards and continued to hang on for life I managed to make it to the next balcony I bumped straight in to my neighbours I had never met them as I forced my way in as I let my self in to there home I was able to walk straight through with out a sound or a word of complaint, still armed I asked her not to shout or make a sound I kissed the lady on the side of her face to say thank you I left the lady side only to go back down stairs to meet the two gang members who looked if they were having a good time as they had smashed my home I thought I heard something fall and smash when I was in the apartment above. As I walked in as I was saying two faced double crossing sons of a bitches, my own boys as I raised my gun as I came from behind the door, it was one of the twins Luke. I was ten times faster then him and ended him by putting a bullet through his chest. He hit the deck with out a sound he was dead. As I moved close to the body kicking his gun aside, I shot him once more to make sure that he was dead. I was now focused on Daniel as I pushed my own apartment door open slowly while leading with my gun I was looking for him as he was looking for me. he was not there where I inspected him to be.

Then I found him I had my gun to the back of hiss head he was shocked with my presents as I pushed the gun in to him. He was talking and talking quickly as he try's to talk himself out of the situation, it was not going to work.

Benjamin:" Drop your gun".

Benjamin had told him, the dog was a little nervous. Benjamin continues.

Benjamin:" So dog you like heights, drop your gun".

Daniel:" Er not really".

Benjamin:" You will tonight".

Benjamin tells the dog to move towards the ledge of the balcony the dog was a little reluctant and is promoted by Benjamin who pushes his gun further in to his back with the words move.

Daniel is still talking Benjamin continues to answer him but in a different way, Benjamin continues you can jump off or you can take a bullet. Daniel knows that he has lost Benjamin raises his gun to the back of Daniels head. Daniel jumps and it is all over.

CHAPTER

SEVENTEEN

EDIT

I needed to move around I was finding out that it was un cool of that fact that I could be found rather than doing the finding it was the other way round of what was supposed to be. I thought about the thought s that entered my mind. I was on the run yet again and on top of that it was from my self. After I had cleaned up the mess that was in my door and on the floor outside and down stairs Daniel was still alive and fighting for his life. He looked like he was extremely badly damaged state so I left it at that. I ws not totally heartless I called him a ambalance. I had decided to go home if I could find my fathers address, then I changed my mind. I did not want to bring the past home with me, at that point I realized that I was being , I decided to lay low for a couple of days. Hoping that I would not have to travel in to my mind or have any dreams.

I was worried I knew that if I was to stay around the rest of the posy would eventually turn up. As I looked around for answers the thought had left my mind I was expecting another visit. The boys would want to know where there boys were. The only answer that I had was that they were dead I could hardly tell them that I threw one of them out of my window. At that point I realized that I really needed a change of the scene. I decided to go for a walk in to town I was not going there to buy clothes or do a little window shopping I was going there to hide, I would feel a lot better with people around at this point.
I was scared with the truth and the things that I had been experiencing for the last couple of months, it all accounts.
I was outside, I could of taken a bus, but again in an instants I changed my mind and decided to take my car. As I opened the car door it sounded like a car. This particular car had never been driven the engine sounded fresh as I buckled myself in strapping the seat belt across myself. I was ready to go. I pushed the ignition button and reeving the engine for a few minutes.

Just as I was warming the car I heard a click I looked in the rear view mirror it was darel, his words were.

Darel:" do not move if you do you are dead".

Benjamin:" you do not have the bottle to pull that trigger and kill me".

Darel:" do not push the push you might end up dead".

As darel pushes the gun further in to his back .

Darel:" do not worry there will be no noise it is a silencer".

That did not make Benjamin feel any better in his situation. as Darel lifts his gun up over the seat and continues the conversation telling Benjamin that he is wanted dead. Benjamin reply's that he already knows.

Benjamin :" So wants knew I know that you know".

Darel:" I know that you know".

Benjamin :" you said the same as me, do not do it".

Darel realizes Benjamin' s position and he cannot move in his position.

It was Benjamin's time to talk knowing that he has a gun to his back he choses to chose the right words. He closes his eyes and is looking for the way out he finds a way but it is not as simple as he might of thought. He goes into his mind entering darels mind Benjamin takes control not only himself but darel too. Benjamin is now outside of the car and is telling darel to get out and step aside, once he is in the open darel is told to drop his arm he does. Benjamin gets back in to the car as he turns the ignition back on. He drives off leaving darel in a disturbing state thinking how he let Benjamin escape.

Benjamin's happy and shouts out that it was an edit as he slaps his hand s down on to the steering wheel as he shouts out the word edit because of what he just experienced one he was happy and feeling good about himself. Benjamin got away from his murderer as Benjamin closes his eyes still while driving extremely fast not worrying for the first time. He was looking for a place of peace he finds the opposite which in his mind was quite usual the more he searched for it the less he seemed to get. Everything was now playing on Benjamin's mind it was clear that he needed a rest as he closed es his eyes again hoping that he would be able to stay put and not travel, but in the end Benjamin gives up as it looked like his mind was taking control of things he ws thinking that if he was going to travel he might as well travel he could not argue as he did not know how to. In the end Benjamin gave up. on this occasion he had found a safe place to be, I realized when he closed his eyes nothing was moving I was at last at a place of peace I was happy and content although I was a little out of my comfort zone I was happy for now.

CHAPTER
EIGHTEEN
THE BURNT
OUT

As I sat down after all the experiences I was burnt out I
could not do anything as I tried to find a way I lacked
the energy to find myself. I was going nowhere I laid on
my sofa looking at the dead body one of my men one of
the gang I out him in the hall way it was another bad
dream. All I had to do or should I say left to do was the
clearing up. I was thin king what I was going to do with
the body. This ws the topic of the day, how do you get
rid of a dead body. I had killed him and left him in my
home. as I hauled the body down stairs passing another
one. I could not remember who was who the one I
threw out of the window was no longer around so I
presumed that the
ambalance had turned up. As for the body in the
hallway he was in a mess also. As I turned him over to
look at his face, It was not mark the dog as I presumed
at first it was Daniel the dog I got there names mixed up

and when they were both alive it normally would happen any way that was that.

I did not care.

As I ws now putting a message out and the thought of it killing my own street gang I had to ask myself the question was I out of my mind. Things on that side were not getting any better. The more that I thought of it the worst it seemed to be. The only escape for me at that time was to close my eyes only to move in to the future or even more so the past.

It was my choice it was a extremely hard to decide a place back or forwards in the end it was not my decision it was like it chose for me. As I closed my eyes once more and within a few seconds I was there. I was in the future once you are in you can not open your eyes unless you want to come back. This was true I had tried even though you may have the feeling that your eyes are open that is when you are back to the beginning.

As I made another attempt to take my mind on a journey after finding the first and second time failed that my third attempt I would make it, I did. I was happy and I was lucky that I had found away. although at this point I was thinking about returning straight back in to the past. I ended up in the future

Many things had changed and when I saw where I was in ws well in to the future like ten years everything had changed I mean everything. It was like a scene from a sci -fi movie, space car and street vendors and most of all the police they were dressed differently like in leather, I could not believe it, as I was standing looking at everything and taking the whole thing n to my mind. Absorbing it all in. I was standing on the street corner on the left hand side of me were people lots of them so many that I was bumped and pushed in to the gutter I was shocked as I chose to ignore it at first then I realized that my wallet had been lifted, I was no fool I felt her hand s touch me, however before she had a chance to run off I had grabbed her. Pulling her aside staying close to her, as I was holding her tightly.

As the girl try's to pull her self saYing the words get off Benjamin grips her tighter. What she calls out stopping the crowd Benjamin gets some funny looks. The police intervene.
Police officer:" what's the problem".
Benjamin smiles.
Benjamin:" Oh nothing I seemed to have lost my wallet".
The girl:" that's right I saw it on the floor I was just returning it to this gentleman".
Police office:" okay there is nothing to see move along".
A conversation starts with the girl and Benjamin as she still has one hand on Benjamin wallet.
Benjamin pushers towards him again he speaks quietly to her and tells her to give it back only to annoy the police officer again. The girl was content in believing that the wallet was hers and refused to bow down in letting go of it. as the police officer approaches them

again Benjamin has no choice but to let go of his wallet it was now hers and in her jacket. The girl was full of acts she now pleads with the officer to let her go Benjamin still has one hand on her.

Police officer:" let the girl go".

Benjamin removes his hand. As they talk themselves out of being arrested Benjamin grabs the girl pulling on her jacket and find s the wallet the police man see s another incident and tells them both to move. Benjamin and the girl agree and start walking, the girl and Benjamin had broken the ice and were talking. As Benjamin looked at his wallet he realizes that the wallet that he has in front of him was not his wallet only to find out later that she was an actual pick pocket and she was welding three other wallets in her jacket eventually after a brief discussion Benjamin finally get his wallet back. The girl pushes Benjamin as they talk Benjamin finds out that the girl was living on the streets. That explained why she was steeling. Benjamin did not believe her and he had other business to attend to. The is looking at Benjamin in a way like she had met him before then they both click she knew him she continues as Benjamin had no idea of what she was thinking. The girl continues that she has seen him before and that it was him Benjamin pauses and asks her who does she think he is.

I came to the conclusion that I had to change my future it was not going to be easy.as I found that my old street gang were looking at the same as me trying to figure the gift out it would only be a matter of time before they solve it, I had control for the moment.

The girl did not want to really know and had walked straight in to it. all thought she was forty years ahead of me and looked like she oozed knowledge I felt kind of sorry for her. She was clearly innocent. But however she cold see right through me. I wanted to befriend her and maybe her advise would help me form the future that I could take back in to the past. May be my advice to her might help change her mind. I aske her if she was hungrey she said that she was. I was not surprised and she asked for chicken. I was surprised that the little bird still existed.

Apart from the stolen wallets in her jacket she told me that there was a food van not far from where we were. I agreed and told her to lead the way. The girl took the lead as we walked through the packed streets I asked her name she said it was Lucy. I was surprised I knew a Lucy once. In return I told her my name. she turned around ion shock after I said Benjamin.

That's weird she said I asked why she said that her brothers name is Benjamin. Lucy walks off the street ahead of Benjamin , he loses sight of her but finds her again after bumping and walking around people. He takes a street corner finding her at the burger stall. Lucy greets the man it was obvious that she had been there before they spoke like they knew each other. Benjamin finally joins her at the bar telling her that he thought that he had lost her and complimenting her stealth, Lucy orders some food not just for her self but for Benjamin also. I was telling her that I was not really hungrey but she seemed to think other wise. Noodles and chop sticks she says as she hands a bowl of noodles to me.

I had no choice but to eat I did not want to disappoint her. The girl was feeling talkative and we were well in to the second course and first conversation since we had met out of the blue she said something and still to this day I remember it. a we spoke the words through our minds the food that I was eating came right out of my mouth on to the floor across the bar and on to another person as clasps for air Lucy ws looking at me as if to say what handing me a glass of beer to help the food that was left in my mouth wash down. I asked her to repeat what she had said her answer to that was what part my answer to her answer was all of it.

Lucy as looking confused and continued like she did not know what I ws talking about. She was playing dumb. Knowing that she had said something wrong but not wrong in Benjamin's eyes, it was information.

Benjamin looks at Lucy trying to gather the information that ws around her.

Lucy:" What".

Benjamin:" nothing".

Lucy:" eat up the food is good".

Benjamin:" what are you".

Lucy:" if you are referring to the way I eat I am a monster, I have not eaten for a few days".

Benjamin:" where do you come from".

Lucy:" you are right I am from the future".

Benjamin:" This is not real is it".

Lucy:" this is it is very real".

Benjamin:" how did you find me, it was destiny".

Lucy:" no your well off".

Benjamin grabs Lucy angrily   and continues to question her as he removes her noodles from her.

Benjamin:" You knew did you not that you was going to meet me, who sent you to me".

Lucy stays silence pulling the noodles back across the table towards her self.

Benjamin believes that Lucy was holding his secret in side her mind he believed that she knew his ways. He goes to get up to leave. Lucy reply to Benjamin leaving her side and tells him that she would catch up with him later Benjamin tells her clearly that the evening was over he was leaving. Benjamin reply to that was he did not think so. She calls out to him again I bet Lucy wanted the last word.

Benjamin could clearly see Benjamin was not in the mood for games and just let the girl win on that occasion.

Benjamin:" See you around".

Lucy's continues to answer him back drawing him back to her she was in control and Benjamin was losing his mind.

Benjamin:" do you always have to have the last word". Benjamin sits back down next to her as he is finishing his bowl of noodles. He continues.

Benjamin:" what is it".

The girl tells Benjamin the truth.

Lucy:" I can see and I can see as far as you".

Benjamin frowns and continues

Benjamin:" then you know why I am here".

Lucy:" I know that you started life off in a hard place no family , money and the money that you made came from deals and then you found the gift after killing your own men cousin and family and on top of that they used what you taught them against you only to force you in to a position that you did not like so you killed them and then you were driven out of your mind continuously after experimenting your own people who turned against you again and it repeated its self on you. That is how far I see. you were calling out you were calling to me. you wanted my help because you did not understand the mind you needed my help.

155

Benjamin:" What are you are you some kind of machine a computer, a fairly wait you're the fairly godmother what you get in my head and start making my wishes come true, what are you going to do". Lucy:" Stop ok I am here to help you I am here to guide you I have been watching you for some time I have been waiting for you waiting to meet you it is not what you can do for me but what I can do for you.

The girl Lucy pushes the bowl of noodles back into Benjamin's direction Benjamin takes a seat and watches, as she finishes her meal Benjamin awakes. But not in two thousand and eighteen well and further in to the future further than the future that he was just in. everything was the same he awakes in his apartment the only thing that had changed was that it seemed bigger some how. He pulls out a smoke they were different they tasted different they were short and just different. Benjamin is control and nice and awake he is being level headed which makes a change. When he looks out side it looked like his street it was small and quiet it ws not like the town centre, he looks up at the sky it is blue he watches the clouds for a moment he checks the time it ws exactly twelve o'clock mid day it nice and light he checks his phone it is not charged. And again of course it was time that he was paid a visit. Somehow his business had followed him. Benjamin was left to figure the rest out for himself travelling through the mind who would think of it. but now his problems of the past have ended up in the future. he continued to think about the experience as he does he finds answers to his problems and questions none of this was real it was all in his mind, but as Benjamin finds himself stuck in the future he begins to think that it was real. He was finding hard to get around it. his thought were racing he wanted to take it to the chalk board he was no time traveller, it was just in his mind he was different he try's to convince himself. There were no machines in evolved it ws purely human his brain.

As Benjamin closes his eyes I was back in my mind I always came back. When he had awoke I was in my bed I awoke sitting up right in shock the pace that I had just taken myself was something quite extraordinary I thought. I wanted to visit it again I wanted to talk to Lucy again weather I can find her or not Benjamin could say right away but he was going to give it a try.

As when Benjamin awoke completely I knew that he had found a totally new world it ws in the mind, what dangers it has I only had the time to experience them it was addictive and a lot of the time I was saying to myself that I was blind, blind to myself and blind to my mind. But in fact it was the opposite my visions were becoming alive even though as I sat down weighing up the pros and cons of this amazing discovery. It seemed that Benjamin had found away in to a knew world. This time it ws anew to me no more steeling or crime even gang warfare was now on a low time score there was nobody to threaten nobody it was at peaceful place for me. it was a good thing although like I said I had brought my problem s from the past with me. now the future the same people with the same problems, I needed a break and it was not a break in my mind as much as I loved the idea, of moving through my mind I had woken up. I was in my apartment on the top floor waiting for that knock on the door it was funny even as I thought about it.

CHAPTER

NINETEEN

TEN WAYS TO DIE

I was seriously hoping that I was going to stay alive, within the next few days the would be four attempts on my life I could not believe as I watched the images I could not believe this was in my mind. Although in saying that it could have been true. Either so I needed a safe place to go. To sit and chill. And I think about what ws actually going to happen. As I closed my eyes as away of escaping the thought, away of escapism I found my self on the same place as I looked back I was some kind of criminal god, it did not feel it. ten attempts on my life within the last four weeks and more to come. I was worried that they would get me. I had no where to hind to make it worse the men were employed by me according to he images that I had been watching. As I tried to figure it out. Why I was hiding in an old travel lodge I had taken myself there it was the only place that I could relax in. The question was what I was doing there I was in my mind thinking about where I was going to next. But something felt wrong. I find out that I employed some body to kill me, I was faking my death and they were on there way I did not know about this the images were there but the answers were not. When I leaped out of the future back all the way back in to the future I was back way ahead of myself. About a year, I was watching my past. Within a few minutes I had stopped watching the past I was back into the future. there ws something about the past that dew me to it maybe the future ws so dull which I found out it was not people tended to think about the past it was safer. As the past already exists it was easier thinking of the past, it was just a theory. There was something I did not like about the past but that was just me. when I awoke I realized that I was or had a conversation as I awoke for the first time talking to my self.

I had awoken in the late evening it was twenty forty, I was surprised that I had not been followed back and I was aware but could do nothing about the visitors that were on there way. I still had the girl on my mind and I wanted to know her I still had some questions to ask her as I was running in to confusion.

When I had looked back in to the past their had been about ten attempts on my life as I looked at each attempt, I thought that I was lucky to be alive. as I looked at the images and it was time to weigh up the facts it was true that I ws not scared but I knew that I was a wanted man. Either way they were going to find me. I had made plans to hide the plans were thought threw but were not as good as they seemed. I would think I was running out of time I was running out of places to hide. I ws left thinking of myself if I had a million dollars I would probably resolve my slight predicament.

In fact I was telling the truth I did have that kind of money in my account but I never thought of paying them off. Mind you that ws a good idea but I knew they would m take the money and run and the whole thing would start over again I was not going to let them bleed me dry. It was not going to happen.
The only thing I wanted at that point was a bed I was outside looking in to the forest listening. I was sitting down on the rocking chair I always thought that I would retire here it was a beautiful place. It was not like I was looking for trouble. It seemed that it always to finds me. Benjamin is back in to his old ways worried for awhile slowly dreaming again he had seen his own murder he was worried that some of the visions that he was having were going to come true. This ws not good in

Benjamin's eyes Benjamin was actually acting normal he was scared the more that he thought about the more worse he slowly became. Benjamin needed a chill pill as closing his eyes was not enough. As he closed his eyes to prepare himself for them he did not want to experience what he was going to experience in the mind.

Benjamin knew that he was on the run and could of told himself this right from the start right from the beginning, it took him a long time to realize this. Benjamin looks upwards knowing that he ws in trouble he looks for god. He stand up he is y=trying to listen to his surrounding trying to look with his mind that's when Benjamin loses it only by an inch Benjamin takes a look at his mind it looked like his preys have worked for one minute exactly after losing control he bring himself totally back together.

I was looking back at the weeks events one I had been shot at quite a lot in my own carpark two I had been thrown out of my of my apartment window and landed in a pool. Four masked men had tried to pick a fight three I had been run over eight I was just about to discuss it with you. I had enough of life and I was desperately think why I should not of gone aboard the holiday was great. I was not heading anywhere. I knew a pilot that possibly might be able to get me there safely. It was just an idea. I was thinking that I might have enough to smuggle myself out , out for good the pilot was a Lear pilot and I knew he could fly. It was done as I made the arrangement , this all happened very quickly as it was fresh in my mind. It seemed the right thing at the time only for one thing I had lost my bottle to fly I ws to scared to board the plane even when he asked and told me it had been al checked out. We did not jet up and we were not on our way America can kiss its arse good bye along with my idea of flying there.

As Benjamin is busy avoiding his thought mainly as they were all about his life. He recalls that he had been killed about ten times Benjamin wants to know who he is running from. As at this point he did not know exactly. It was playing ion his mind.
Benjamin is chilled he knows that he has got a rough time ahead of him. It was a kind of thought that Benjamin had right from his beginning I was dying I closed my eyes and got the answers to everything. This sent me all the way back there was to many laws. I kind of thought with everything I was dying I closed my eyes getting the answers that I needed to protect myself further in to the future. there ws something wrong I sensed this earlier something had changed in our minds the future was about to change which changes everything it must of came from our past.
Somebody ws trying to hail me the first time was enough as it was so intense I did not want to feel that way again I ws left unable to speak or communicate for at least an hour I thought somebody had slipped me something except there ws nobody around to do that, it was the same old stuff cold sweats and other things. I will leave the rest for your imagination.

It was a scary experience as again when I recovered I closed my eyes again only to fall flat on my face there was nobody there something was definatly happening I needed to find out what. I was thinking what was going on, at this point I decided to call on my friends I did not have to many tat I still would talk to most of them had left and the rest of them were probably out with family as such probably getting high I know they did as I used to. I did not mean neighbours I ws talking about that bond true friends they were with me within the day even though they were gangsters also they were like brothers the meeting with them took me way back as we all remenising about the playing in the park and old times.

I was giving it to them straight as they were to me in the end I hid nothing I told them the whole thing I ws happy to in there company as they were mine.

As time settled so did my mind I had decided to give myself some space for the next two months I ws in my garden but again the problems started over again I ws not getting on wit the company that housed me there company was getting to personal and I could not do the things that I wanted to do they were employed to look over me well that what there flyer said when I picked it up. the things that I wanted to do they were extremely strict and I thought I would be better on my own again I just had to break the news to them. I was disappointed as I asked them to leave they did not understand and they all looked in shocked when I put it across to them that they were all fired.

I was back on the street again as for my friends advice well you know how that turned out.

I wanted to be there it was not the first time I looked at it as a challenge some you win and hopefully you would go on winning. You could actually learn a lot from being homeless it ws all about respect. I knew what was to come the first thing I did was buy a big sleeping bag one that I could carry, the second was to walk in order that somebody would find me I had a couple of options left the last of them was to sleep in a shop doorway it was a good disguise as nobody noticed me I was a tramp.

CHAPTER TWENTY
LOCKED OUT

As I sat in the doorway I was looking up at the sky's they were changing fast one moment there was clouds which seemed to be moving fast there ws an eclipse I supposes you could call it that although it came over cloudy then nothing, just the darkness I was reasonably paranoid anyway on the simple fact that I was still alive I closed my eyes thinking what a=was to come next, and what I was to make of this as I did the light of the moon came back with more darkness and clouds over took the sky's. and a storm started.

I was not in the best of places and I could feel the cold chill for the first time of the fresh air.   The small door was not going to be enough to keep me from the weather which was a head.

It started to rain. I was stuck the small door was not enough to protect me. the lightening and thunder came next the crushing sounds echoed everywhere I was thinking was the weather always like this, it was getting more and more exciting. I was watching the sky's the flashing lights of what I presumed ws aircraft in the sky above.

After an hour or so the storm finished with hail stones. I was drenched all the way through even though the storm as the storm moved. I decided to move myself somewhere a little bit more comfortable there was some woods close by. I always thought that it was a forest it started to rain heavy I could see the woods it was made as part of a park as I entered the park closer to my destination as this came to my mind as I was thinking about a

my where about I had lost all sense of direction as the rain hit my face I could not see where I was going. I found a bench I was thinking that you do not get benches in forests maybe you did.

Even though I was still outside as the storm resides I found myself on te park bench it ws quite peaceful and that is all I wanted and I could lay down I was impressed that my face fitted on to the bench arms, and I fitted the bench. I did not know the name of the park that I was in it ws far from home that is all I knew but within walking distance. But it was not over yet from nowhere I heard something smash, I did not move a muscle I was a little cautious and held my ground until I heard the voices, it was dark and I could not see, I still stayed put having too, I could hear people but I could not see them. I looked in to my pocket and felt around I had a lighter I then produced a cigarette from the pocket it was all I had for a decoy as I lit the smoke up and placed on the floor half lit hoping that they would find it instead of me as I turned the smoke around looking at it from all angles as they would hoping that the smoke was facing the right way I made off in the opposite direction.

I then emptied the lighter of the fluid and threw it away, I was listened to it hit the ground and I ws off I started to run. And it sound ed if they had found the cigarette I was lucky I was not to far away from the town centre as I made it to a car park a place that I knew I could drive which was a bonus I new that I had to be quick and quiet. As for the people who I did not know I think that they took my bate. As I got in to the car I was hotwiring it rather quickly. I broke the window quietly to get in forcing a large noise they would hear it by the time they pin pointed me I would be long gone. I was quiet as I was meant to be.

As I drove off past a number of people I ws thinking that they were all looking for me. as they were walking in my direction. As I slammed on the gas as I tired to pull away I was not thinking about the car I just put my foot down. It was quicker than I thought.

I was hoping at that I had time to make a quick getaway but in fact the opposite happened I ended up reversing going backwards extremely fast as I tried to find the gears. Straight out of third in to reverse looking to slow down as I was moving quickly there was a bump and then another one. I was sure that I had run over something. at that point in time I did not care I just wanted to get away from the crowd. I guess I just wanted to get away. I did not look back my consciousness was clean. I did not see anything. As I tried to find the right gear to drive in with that kind of pressure it ws not easy to do. I was now moving in the right direction away from the crowd. After I had escaped in to a small lay by, in fact out side ta council block I was feeling and getting more frustrated I remembered the words , I could throw somebody out of a window within that second there was a loud crash it landed on the car bonnet some body had fallen from the building and they had landed right on the bonnet. There ws a big dent and the window screen had a massive crack in it. as I looked in shock I was thinking I was better of in my mind. I did not know who the victim was all I know was that it came from way up there I did not get out of the car. I was going to make my way home.

I was caught up in two worlds at this point there was two options one go upstairs and pay the mans respect for him or do a runner I waited in did the runner. I decided that I did not want to get involved from that point of the manhating the deck although I did think

168

about somebody would probably do the same to him everybody gets to pay in the end. No man or women is immortal its bollocks all that stuff on TV, As I moved quickly through the night knowing that the car that I had stolen was now part of a crime scene. I made my way on foot hoping that I was heading in the right direction, trying not to think about what happened I can say for sure I will not go out sleeping in parks again it ws not a good experience t=for me. I needed a disguise I rolled my jeans up making it look like I was out on a run. That was extremely hard to I had run about half a mile I was tired. I had already thrown away my jumper and lost my jacket which I forgot to tell you about in the park. I now looked like I was on a run t-shirt and shorts. I already had the shoes on. No problem. It was my mistake to throw away my jumper I could not stop thinking about somebody else finding it would lead straight to me in time. Especially my drink as I moved slower believing that I ws now in the safer part of the town I decided tom stop for a breath I was leaning and trying to catch my breath at tat moment everything seemed to be fine technically. Apart for that poor fellow the memory hit me hard why was I scared I use to do things like that all the time back in the day. I was losing it I was sure. As I grasped for some more air, I could here the sound s in the back ground. They were sirens I did not know if they were getting closer or further away. I was convinced by my own knowledge that we would be meeting soon I continued to run slowly they were heading for me for sure but what direction were they going to come from I was soon to find out. I licked my finger holding it to thee wind to find out which direction was north. It made a difference in what direction I was going to go in.

I took off again this time heading in the opposite direction, I was cool as the police car slowly drove past me I was in the clear again I got it wrong only for the fact that I was heading in the same direction as them even worse they stopped to offer me a lift as they slowed down pulling up next to me, it was as I expected I knew exactly what was going to happen.

As I took off again heading in the opposite direction I was as cool as I could have been I was as cool as the police itself. The police car slowly pulls up past me. I was thinking I was in the clear again for that fact that I was heading towards the destruction that I had created and the police car behind me were piling up.
I knew exactly what I was going to do. I could see it clearly what was going to happen. I thought I was in the clear in fact it it was the opposite at that moment the police pulled me over I said to the officer Benjamin:" What".
He looked at me as I just looked at him. We were still moving he was in his car I was slowly bunny stepping I was soft footing it just to keep up with the car why was I following them I did not know he looked over to me again and pointed to the ground and then he spoke.
Police officer:" your shoe lace is undone".
He drove off leaving me looking at the un done shoe. I thanked him as he drove off I got to my knees and did the shoe up tightly, as I was slowly panting and gathering my breath I said to my self are the police as really think and kind as that.
As I got my breath back by the look of things I had got away, now I was in a different part of town, I was only a few streets away from the crime to close for my

likening I turned around and wanted to run away further only to shout and to walk home.

As I neared my home and as I walked in to the apartment block I did not realize that I had my phone on me as I felt it vibrate I did not answer it straight away as I never took the vibration as it was not important as in anybody that I would know just business however if it actually rang I would have probably answered it. clever using two tones. I left it for exactly a minute that way I knew that if it was important who ever was on the other end meant to get in touch other wise it would be left ringing or I would click on and hang up. also I knew that it would be somebody that I knew. It was all just safety precaution's. I also knew that it would be somebody that knew me.

I was fed up with life and wanted a knew one I wanted to leave the city alone no more killing no more street crime no more bank robbery's, and I wanted to go straight. I wanted to keep it to my self and as it was me and as it was me I did not think it could be that hard. The phone kept on vibrating I knew that it was somebody who knew me. I turned my phone off. Only to accidently re push the re-dial button I felt the phone vibrate thinking nothing of it at that point I was getting in to the lift always getting paranoid as I set the journey upwards by pressing the top floor button mine was at the very top it was the en suite apartment I could not get the idea that there would be somebody waiting there for me I took a deep breath as I watched the electronic dial count the floors going upwards. The paranoid feelings were still there. If there was anybody there at all the lift doors open slowly at that point I did not know which was scary the lift doors opening or going up to the top floor or even worse the long stairs case that crawl upwards along side the large panelled windows of the building.

When I had got all the way to the top I had a long door to walk through until I came to my front door again I had the same feeling of paranoia coming over me. I pushed my key in to the door looking over my left shoulder as if some body was there in fact I had a habit of doing this where I picked it up I do not know. I opened the door closing the door behind me as I opened it again taking a cheeky look again just to make sure that I was alone. I stayed there for exactly a minute making sure that I was alone as I finally shut my door and finally felt a little more normal I stepped inside closing the door behind me.

Not putting the lights on straight away which would not be normal I checked my door again this time looking through the spy hole. Nothing I was happy and even more relaxed.

Noticing as I walked to check another door and windows, that I had my jeans still rolled up from the run in with the police something that I had forgotten the police man did not notice, lucky. I pushed the door closed and turned on all the lights I moved to my kitchen to make myself a cup of tea I was thinking about that day I had a good time I thought but it had its troubles, I would sleep that off. After I had turned the kettle off slowly flipping the switch pushing the kettle away from myself on the side I moved back to my lounge I sat down on my couch as I put the drink to my mouth taking a small sip more of a slurps I was happy to be home.

For once in the last few years I finally got some proper sleep for reason something had changed no visons no traveling through my mind for once I was having a peaceful time.

I was thinking that I was in the future was going to have the chance to enjoy my life, after a few days and a couple of nights of just sleep I was leaving the things that bothered me the most behind, I had no remorse of the things that I had done in the past and I thinking that I might find away out of all the things that I had done I n the past, you know all the bad things I ws not repentant or sorrow full. It was not for me it was for them. that thought stayed with me for sometime maybe I should be thinking about what I had thought would or could be the other way around. It was a stupid but interlecual thought but it never looked at that or those thoughts like that before I suppose it was just life.

This time I was awake I awoke slowly as usual and I woke up with a little smile on my face I awoke happily I closed my eyes again just to make sure that I was not dreaming I was here. As usual I make myself a cup of tea and went up stairs and outside on to my roof it was quiet and peaceful time not just for me but again I felt that something had changed I had for one, but it seemed to me that it was not just me but it was the shape of my mind. I felt different but I looked the same, my behaviour had changed I was doing things differently and doing things that I would not normally do. I was absorbing everything I did in to my mind. And I mean everything, I would look at the sky differently thinking about how beautiful it actually was in the early evening's I never really noticed it before that point. My neighbours had changed they would pass me by and actually say hello. It was just the little things like that were making me good. I was thinking that I had changed or somebody had changed something to Have me thinking this way. What I was experiencing was real. Except I had nobody to tell.

As I was taking it all in I did not know that things were going to change fast I wanted more of those experience's that had happened in the last few weeks to continue unfortunately things began to fall apart it had stated again. I did not believe things as a circle was made I thought that I ws on the straight and narrow. But that thought had been lost and I knew that it was not coming back it started while I was asleep I was dreaming of being arrested it only gets worst form there I was cold sweats they had started again I was waking up in puddles of it the drooling I was losing it, all I could do was try and sleep it off the symptoms got worse and were getting worse. At first I thought it5 was flew or some kind of cold. How wrong I was, it had started to travel through my mind. Again the vision were back sucking me in, then I saw it the future again. The cold if it was a cold left me one morning as I woke I continued the morning as I continued every morning with tea not knowing were I had been or what I had been doing.

Then nothing I was normal again, at the first at that point the point of remembering I had past out on my breakfast bench in my kitchen I did not know where I was or how long I had been there for as I awoke again for the second time after passing out again this time I had found the memory. As I awoke I woke in shock like everything was not as everything should be it was like I had been dead, I had no memory of this. As theses thoughts occurred I knocked my tea over on to the floor I was watching but in slow motion. I joined it soon after. I had lost my mind. How did that happen within that thought as I made a cup of tea again just awaking up I quickly, properly, unconsciously made it to the toilet as I pulled the toilet lid up managed to completely miss it only to puke up in to the bath room sink. I past out again I was counting the minutes In my mind something was happening. This time when I had awoke I was in the future through my mind. I had travelled all the way in to the future.

CHAPTER TWENTY

ALL THE WAY BACK

When I awoke I ws in the park for the same strange reason I was in there last time I was drawn to the place it seemed. I was paranoid it did not have that usual feeling it was an odd one. And in that thought did not want to be there. The question was why I was in the park and whom I was suppose to meet I did not think at that time that I was going to meet anybody I just presumed it not thinking that it could be for a completely different reason. I was in my normal place sitting down, it was getting late and getting later I wanted to stay but mind was tired in the end I met nobody, and I made my way back.

When I opened my eyes I was at home I was thinking that the journey had been a complete waist of my time what was I trying to do or even more to the fact what was I doing. When I opened my eyes I checked the time it was late morning about half past eleven. I was going to have to wait until the late evening until I got another chance to go all the way back which in fact was all the way forwards, as much as I would of liked to say that I was feeling fine I was not in fact I was feeling rather sick. I was feeling drained I was concerned.

Not a little but a lot I was not sure of the effects of the traveling was doing to my mind, I did not look any different or feel any different.

I already knew not to think about what I was experiencing but I could discuss it with thinking. I knew not to speak about it as through other experiences that it is the mouth that always seems to get me in to trouble if I did not say it then there was the chance that there is nobody to hear it. I had no problems in keeping my experiences to myself.

I was looking in from the outside enjoying the view and I was surprised now far 9 could actually see. as I looked over the town that was in front of me and beyond the trees that polity blocked the view.

As I looked upwards towards the sky I could see the moon just in its place. The clouds were moving slowly form down here but in fact they were moving extremely fast from up there the world was turning and I was not going to be left behind. As I have already explained that I could travel through the mind. I was now looking at the future but on this occasion I had decided to go back in to the past. in side of my mind there was lots of question that I needed to ask weather I got the answer that I wanted was a different question all together. When I thought I was going forward in fact I was going back I had set my self up going , moving back in to the past.

While pushing my mind to the limits as I looked at each memory I was watching a totally different experience from travelling forwards, I found out that I could stop time.in my mind this was a knew occurrence I was not sure weather it was a warning or if it normal for that state of my mind it meant something I needed to know what. This lead me to believe tat I could take images form the past and put them in to the future the question was could it be reversed. But however this ws only theory for now I did not know why I was shown this I certainly did not understand this. It ws something that I would take up in the future. As I delt with the moving images of the past I suppose you could call them scenes other things like objects it was like I was reliving all my mistakes that I had made way back when I was younger some people say you cannot change the past only for remembering it was a shame though because I was could and I was.

It was strange to me at first that particular moment that I went back into the park. This time it was day time but in my mind it was night time darkness as I was keeping a low profile I found myself sitting down on the short grass it was as green as green grass could be it was a large field obviously as I was in a park there were people all around and dogs and people playing and it was noisy. I could see myself and I wanted a closer look I wanted to approach myself for a conversation I wanted to send myself a message so I would know in the future.

As I looked hard at myself then looked even harder at my actual self I knew that I already knew. As I looked at him he looked back at me it was like we both knew. At that point I was distracted a frizz be landed near me I picked it up and held for a second it felt real I there it back to the people that were playing with it. when I had looked up to look at myself again I had left. Benjamin had brought himself back leaving the memory in the past and slowly awakes in the future where he ws suppose to be. As Benjamin slowly find s himself in the future as he wakes he is tired , drained out. He is thinking comprehending exactly what he had done in a few days he should receive a message from himself from the past which would join him in the future as he become more awake he falls in shock it ws with what he had done. He knew that he had stumbled across something amazing he had nobody to tell not that it would make a difference the problem was how ws he going to keep it a secret people already knew that he was crazy maybe he would work for himself on his own behalf.

Benjamin was impressed with what he had just experienced and wanted to go outside to clear his mind he had been out of his mind for a few days even though it only felt like a few hours Benjamin walks to his window and looks out side it was still light, just. Again he thinks about what happened last time he went outside he did not think it ws possible for the same thing to happen twice in his situation so soon. The odds were with him on this occasion they were there so he could way up a calculation for his evaluation. He ws not sure he could trust his odds would he be safe. He insisted as he picked up his jacket putting it on and not down as he was preparing him self. For a normal person it would be easy it was just a jacket in Benjamin eyes it was complicated. He was unsure that it would be safe not the jacket but going out side. He insisted that he would be fine to himself as he looks for his door keys. While this is happening he takes off his jacket a number of time s as he is forced to change his mind until he finally wins by ignoring his own decisions. He finds his keys as he picks them up he is forced to put them back down Benjamin knows that he's is playing a game and it is a dangerous one at that.

Benjamin is thinking that it was bad idea as he is having a few problems getting through the door. He checks and double checks that he has his shoes on, He did. Feeling stupid and confused only to make things harder, as he wanted to go outside so much in the excitement he walked out of the apartment leaving his coat and keys behind him locking himself outside as he turns to catch the door just as it slams shut, closed tight he had forgot his keys. Benjamin slams his hands on the door wishing that it would open as he does the sound of his small attack echoes through the door. He stands by his door waiting for the sound of the echo to disperse trying to think of a way in.

Benjamin first thoughts after his little episode was to go to the fire exit, after he goes off to find it he finds that there is no fire exit. He returns back to his front door the second thought was to call a lock smith but at this time of the night he would be surprised if the lock smith would come out. Even more so he had also left his phone in side he thought he had it in pocket he did it was in the pocket of his jacket. It was stupid Benjamin thought.

In the end Benjamin has two more options the first was to kick the door open or continue his walk in to town and deal with being lock out later Benjamin thought about both solutions closely as there was no reason for Benjamin to be inside he decides to walk in to town. He knew that it would be an adventure. So excitement what ever he did. As he makes his way out of the building he had decided that when he gets back he would kick the door in himself problem sloved. He was happy that he had found a simple answer to his simple problem. Benjamin leaves nearing the stairs door he stops as the lift door over the other side of the large hall way stops as it buzzes the light above the door turns it self on before the doors open. Benjamin was lucky as he ws at the other end of the long hall way he thinks instantaneously that it would be trouble that was his paranoia. He quickens his pace not wanted to be seen. He stops at the end of the hallway and stands behind the exit door to glimps as he pears through the door he was right two blokes holding weapons.

Benjamin hides closing the door quietly he stands on the stairs gathering his thought's he takes another peak, he hears one of them speak he tells the man in front of him to take the stairs. Benjamin catches on he was on the run with one hundred flights of stairs as he runs downwards getting faster and faster he moves quickly almost like a child. Trying not to disturb the floor as the echo of this footsteps would give him away as he gets to near to the bottom he is out of breathe stops listening

and knowing that he is being followed he takes a beep
breath and he is off again. Benjamin knows that he is
being followed and takes a detour back into the
building this was his mistake, as he had left the man
behind him a chance of getting closer and it was bad
luck as he nowhere to hide just a door by the fir exit.
The other man was in the lift and it was just turning up
on the same floor that Benjamin was on. Benjamin
takes another big breath, as the lift doors open the man
steps out Benjamin has two choices one was to confront
the man two was to keep running.
Benjamin was in luck as the man was now in front of
him he ws busy checking the rest of the floors
Benjamin sprints down the last set of a few flights of
steps. The man on the steps did not notice Benjamin as
he bumps past him and heads out of the building.
Benjamin escapes the two men and knows not to go
back to his apartment again for a while. There was no
noise as Benjamin walks out side. As he walks off he
still feels the danger, I suppose it was a gut feeling as
he finds a car to hot wire s he breaks in the car with a
brick straight through the window. Waking up the
owner and neighbours as a few lights above were
switched on and the surrounded area was woken. There
was some shouting as Benjamin takes off his t-shirt
rapping around his hand and pulling and pushing the
glass of the dented door on to the floor. He gets in
breaking the steering, after getting in and brushing the
rest of the broken glass off the seat on to the floor.
After pulling the wires out of from under the steering
wheel he hot wire's the car pulling the two wire out and
then touching them together there is a little spark and
the engine starts running he drives off in the direction
of the town. It was night time he could just see he looks
in the rear view mirror, and he was glad to be on his

way. He could see and hear the owner of the car as he was shouting.

I did not realize the type of model the car was and to be honest I did not care until I found out that it was a brand new car it was spanking brand new I only found this out as the engine had not been broken in and when I wanted to be doing sixty I was doing fifteen. Not the fastest way to escape. As I was chugging along I thought that it was fun, it had must have been the slowest get away ever in history. I had to pull over as I had to as there was a motor bike sitting all alone it would be quicker. After I had looked at it I was sure that it had a full tank. This time the journey was a little bit quicker, just. As I changed through it's gears I was heading for the motor way at that point it was the only place I wanted to be. I did not care where I ws going as long as I was going there fast. I knew that it was going to come to an end as I had no keys to the petrol cap, I guess the running out of petrol, was the end of my little joy ride as I came to a stand still in the country side.

I got off the bike quickly leaving it on the road side the hard shoulder on a country road it was left without petrol and the steering lock was broken. I started walking I had no idea where I was. But I had good ears

I was following the sound of another motor way as I was looking for another road I was surprised that the country side was so quiet in fact I was enjoying the walk and it was sonly eight miles to the next village, problem I had no money I had left my wallet with my keys back at the apartment. I did not notice and I should of taken it on the way out side. I was looking for a bed and breakfast, and I stubbled on what I was thinking of. As usual I was going to pull a fast one. I explained to the girl at the reception that my money would be paid to her through a phone call from my bosses who will arrive in the morning, early. As there was only a few hours of the evening left, she agreed and gave me a room and of course I asked for some food and drink but completely forgetting to ask her where I was. She handed me the keys to my room it was modest and I was grateful.

I ate the food which was brought to me and drunk a few beers on top of that. I could not be bothered to looked around I was more concerned how I was going to get out of the bed and breakfast with out paying.

In the morning as the three business men turned up I walked out quickly towards them greeting them the girl at the reception was surprised as she did not known that I had seen them on there guest list the previous day in fact the other night. As I greeted them as if they knew me I managed with ease to remove a wallet and on top of that a set of car keys as Benjamin walks out he is talking.

Benjamin:" Hello welcome, I will go get the bags and park your car up you can pay for the night I will be back in a few minutes".

The three men looked confused I moved so quickly they did not get a chance to speak. I was a perfect pick pocket. The three men were baffled, until I did not re appear and the girl was shouting as she realized that I was pulling a fast one, I got into the driving seat of the car and drove off I could see the looks of there faces, all of them came outside to watch me drive off. The man's who's keys that I had was left with out his wheels like my last victim.

The car's tank was full according to it's petrol gage, and as I looked in side the glove compartment there ws another wallet, and it ws far from empty. I was on my way again not to far from where I was going.

I needed a break from everything my mind stupid to say really as it was in my mind.

As I drove extremely fast with a full tank of petrol I was heading across the country side, within a hour or so, I did not realize that I had driven so far on the bike I did not know where I was. I was not just in the mind but physically. As I came towards a set of traffic lights I could feel it I was being watched it was strange as I looked at the lights, it was a difference feeling, there was something strange, I felt strange. I pulled over taking the keys out of the ignition, I turned around just taking a good look around, as I was taking a good look at the motor cycle I found nothing in the end. I thought it was just me being paranoid as I looked further under the cycle still I found nothing. I looked under the cycle again just to make sure that I did not miss anything. It was me I ws feeling a little bit paranoid. As I got back on to the motor bike I sat there absorbing the whole experience in to my mind. It was midnight when I had awoke slumped across the petrol tank. The roads were busy as ever I stepped off the bike to go to the toilet enough people saw me I did not particularly care in fact there were some cheers which made me smile down upon it. and further beeps from the a few passer by. I had gone all the way it was time to go back. I had enough I wanted to go home.

It was time to mix again with friends and not so good
friends, I had been invited to a party I got the message
not personally but I heard it through the grape vine so I
invited myself it was a change of scene. There was no
invitation and all I knew at the time was the address. I
was going to take a chance, I was thinking that I should
invite myself. So I did. I knew that it would give me the
chance to make up with old friends maybe find some
knew one's.

As I prepared myself for the journey into an extremely
poor part of town. I began to understand some things,
certain things. As I drove I could not get the thought of
meditation out of my mind. And what it was doing to
me it was like a permanent marker.

As I found the home after a good hour of looking for it
I found the address. It must have been the party there
were enough people around on that street. So I
presumed that it was the right address, as I parked up
not to close and not to far from the house that I think
the party was at. As I approached the door pushing my
way through past the drunken door person who was not
a door person and into the hall way filled with people I
could see a few people that I had recognized. As I
turned around the door man had grabbed me taking me
by the arm and grabbing the back of my suit jacket. He
ws not particularly happy and it ws not the first man
that I had met at the door previously. As he pulled me
to the front of the hallway and pushed me through the
only entrance back out side I was thinking he was an
ass for not letting me in. I told him the way that he had
left me feeling. He just looked at me. I stood out side

waiting as I was just turning away thinking that my night was over and it all been a waste of time two men looked over to him and gave him the nod to let me in. The seemed to know me I had no idea who they were. I was happy that they let me in. There was plenty of women there most of them were probably single waiting for there prey. Most of them in my eye were just there to find the next rich guy. As I looked around I ws getting in the mood of the party as I took another drink from the waiter's tray knocking the glass of wine back in the posh glass.

By the time that I ws finished I ws basically and completely smashed off my face and that's when the trouble started accidently bumping in to some guy and knocking his drink over him and to make things worse losing my drink over him at the same time. This time not just removing his drink from his hand but spilling my drink down his suit, tie and shirt.

He looked at me as I looked at him staring as I tired to say sorry it did not impress him.

Stranger:" What do you think you are doing".

Benjamin:" Arrh sorry".

Stranger:" You do not say sorry to me".

There ws a short pause as Benjamin is trying to clear the air.

The bloke that Benjamin was talking too seemed to know him, the man ws obviously angery and makes a move he reaches out to grab Benjamin's jacket but Benjamin was quicker as he ws making an approach at the same time grabbing the mans hand holding it tight until the man yells ok.

Benjamin continues:" I did warn you should so excepted my apology I am sorry about the suit and I am sorry about your tie".

Stranger:" ok I mean I understand apology excepted. Benjamin let's the stranger go as he does the whole party stops just for a second then continues again the man is looking down not knowing where to look. Benjamin took the incident know further as he had other things on his mind. The man walks away the party was coming to an end. Benjamin was thinking an thinking was a problem he was over thinking and thinking why was he at the party he was doing this while he was drunk this only confused his situation only to cause one as he stumbles across the man who trying to kill him.

The man that Benjamin had bumped into was the man that Benjamin was going to kill. It ws funny as he had lifted Benjamin's wallet from his jacket Benjamin thought that it was fine expected that at a least. That he would have a drink as he approached him as Benjamin nears his table the man is sitting at. None of them realized that they were hunting each in the party. And on top of that had never met the question was how did they find him and how did they know that I would come to this party. How did they know that Benjamin would be there.

After that party I had a lot to think about I ws lucky to be able to walk in and out with out being killed. I was not stupid I knew that that bloke recognised me, within a few minutes

 of the end of the party they were behind me. I made it quickly to my car, except the car that I approached was not my car I was looking at the same model except it ws not my car I thought that it had been stolen as I tried the keys none of them on my key ring would not fit. I

190

realized rather quickly that I had forgotten where I had parked. I was looking in the wrong place.

As I looked around not trying not to shout and causing more attention upon myself. I ws thinking that things were not as they seemed and my life was just about to be taking a change for the worst. As I looked in my jacket pocket for my car key's I could not find them although they had not been stolen as my wallet had as I casually eventually found them I pulled them from within my phone pocket from the inside left hand side of my suit jacket. As I pushed my key in to the door of the car. I was thinking that I lucky that they had not been stolen. The cars lights started to flash and within a second it had caused the surrounded car to do the same on top of them some houses alarms started also it was really noisy as I got in to my car under the street lights watching the neighbourhood wake up shouting was heard as bedroom lights came on.

I made a slow get away as I drove off up the street only to the fact that I was still to drunk to drive in fact when I had woken up I was surprised that it was in my own car parked on the side of the road half on the pathway half on some grass. It ws a magical come down not knowing what ws in the actual drinks. It was not like me to complain as I did not feel any different from when I had entered the party as to leave. Only to the point that I had lost my keys. And approaching the wrong car it was obvious that the car was in front all along and some body had poisoned my drink. Thinking about that made me feel ashamed as no body had done anything and I was making excuses for my own behaviour. Somebody ws trying to make me look stupid.

It was true I was coming up some body had spiked my drink as I looked around trying not to shout and bring even more attention to my self. It did not bother me that I was feeling high and had slipped some drug I was waiting for it to start to kick in so I could find out which drug the person had given me. So I could way up the pros and cons of how I was going to bring my self down as I thought about the people that I spoke to on that evening and who was handling my drinks. The old memories were coming back the memories that I had been trying to avoid.

As I was trying to stay with it trying to pull myself together knowing what ever ws in the drinks could not have been of a hard dose and I was sure that I would feel a little more myself by the early evening. As it was now in my system I thought I might as well enjoy it. It was like eating a can off dog food. With out taste but enjoyable as you never know. As I sat down straight after I sat down getting up off the pavement I was trying to think of the substance that I had been given. I would not have taking it myself I had stupidly let myself take it. I never got that far what ever it was, ws the end I was out cold on the cold floor I did not know how long I was going to be there I was still trying to figure out what substance I had been spiked with and where I actually was. I thought I was at the train station for the next twenty hours waiting for a train. When I awoke my vision was blurred and there were some old people around me as I laid on the floor there was some tramp trying to remove my jacket I could feel him pulling on my clothes as he was trying to remove them I ws being robbed. I did not jump at this moment until he snatched my mobile phone as I tried to grab it back half asleep and drooling form my mouth. I managed to snatch my mobile phone back and eventually my car keys. I knew that some body was paying me a visit in a extremely clever way.

A I awoke the tramp looked at me and I looked at the tramp, he knew what I was thinking

Benjamin:" give me my money".

Tramp:" What he replied".

Benjamin gets up o to his feet it looked like he had brought himself back and down. The tramp continues.

Tramp:" I have none, I thought you were dead".

Benjamin:" I want the money old man".

The tramp insisted that he had mistaken Benjamin for a drunk and he had not taken Benjamin for any money just his shoes and socks. Benjamin looked down at his feet it was true Benjamin ws shoeless and sockless.

Benjamin:" great, you did a better job than my boy's, if that is the case empty your pockets".
The tramp hesitates and doe as he his asked he turns out his pockets he only does it because he is afraid of Benjamin. Benjamin is happy to see that the tramp was telling the truth. As Benjamin looks upwards he says the words that there was no trains running today as he looks down noticing that his watch was missing from his wrist.

Benjamin shouts out for a moment and cusses for a few seconds, he looks at his feet and notices that his shoes were missing also. As the train pulls up the tramp has got on, at that point the tramp was in walking distance down the other end of the platform Benjamin could clearly see that he had his socks and shoes on. Benjamin shouts.
Benjamin:" stop, stop that train that tramp has got my shoes on".
Nobody listens and the train does not stop Benjamin is running after the train as the tramp is closing the door and when Benjamin finally catches up he is running out of platform. The tramp is bye the window and as they both notice each other again in a short time the tramp holds up Benjamin's wallet and then his watch.
Benjamin finally catches on he had been done there is a long silent he knows that he has lost, as the tramp just to say good bye give Benjamin the finger.

Benjamin smiles and walks off to find where he can plan his journey home.

Benjamin finally gets home not forgetting about is old friends knowing that he could be walking straight in to danger. Not feeling any different as he walks in to his home. as he nears his front door he can see that it is clearly open. He sops takes a breath and looks in to the darkness of his doorway through the small opening left by he door being opened. He pushes further trying not to make a sound. He try's to push the door open trying not to make a sound. Just behind the door where it had been left open, his old school base ball bat is still there obviously been left un noticed. Lucky he thinks as he acknowledges that it is still there. as he picks it up slowly closing the door behind him. As he gets closer toward the end of his hall way as knows he is in the building. As he nears his living room there is nothing he checks the place out quickly and quietly. As he turns on the lights he can clearly see that his house had been smashed to pieces. Benjamin falls to his knees he was upset. Everything had gone. He knows the game is over his old posy and there new friends were still after him.

Benjamin now feeling even more un settled he did not even look at the damage the mess in his home so bad everything and I mean everything was smashed it had been totally destroyed. He walked across the room there was the window he did not even have to open it, it lead to a balcony there was no curtains on the window they had been blown or thrown over the edge. He walked to his bath room all smashed the toilet too. He walked back to what was his living space e=al of it ripped and broken there would be nothing to sit on. There was nothing left the TV had been un plugged and thrown out of the window on to the concrete floor below. Benjamin ws thinking how ?

Why? He knew that he was still paying his dues. He stops thinking for a few ours he finally bows down to what had happened. He know that he has lost his home. a few hours later he was on his own and on the street again this time it ws not by chose.

Benjamin ws trying hard to stay with it he was starting from the very beginning again he was looking to find a normal life trying to leave the things that he had done and experienced behind himself. He could not live in the town any longer to many memories that was his excuse with everything that had happened he ws thinking a new start would be a good thing. He longed to meditate but something ws telling him to wait with everything that had happened in the last few days. He did not believe that it would matter how wrong he was.

Benjamin grabs what clothes he can he stuffs them in to a spots bag, he takes a look at what was his home once more the destruction in his home was incredible he ws hoping that it was not going to be stuck in his mind it is funny how the images work as he walks around the broken table and smashed glass on the floor and makes it to his front door he was feeling hurt as he picks up a picture. It ws a picture of his father he looks at it once more and places back on the ground with the broken glass frame on to the floor.

He walks out closing the door locking it shut he makes his way down the cooridoor in to he lift this time he is not to concerned but just as scared as usual. As he heads down wards outside at the bottom of the lift doors he steps out in the car park. It is all nice and quiet.

As he steps outside for the first time in the night on the street, he makes his way, Benjamin had a lot to consider even though he had money he was thinking that it might be good thing it reminded him of the old days although back them he thought that he was going somewhere. A place were he used to play as a kid.

The park, he ended up walking the journey was totally different to what he expected. But however he by the morning he was in a new place a totally different place. He had not realized that he had walked so far. He finds a nice quiet door way by a church with benches.

After Benjamin had put his bag down he realizes that he in fact ws actually tired. And only meant to close his eyes for a second. A cat nap, he awakes the next day in the middle of the next day.

Benjamin woke up in a reassuring reasonable good mood, there was a problem that there was very little light. Benjamin was seated down and was in the mood for some meditation.

Benjamin closes his eyes as another journey had begun. He noticed at first that he w as outside his visions as he was outside and when he ws inside his visions would be in side there was an obvious answer to this it just needed to be found. But Benjamin agreed that if that was the way it worked then there is no problem. He had no arguments.

As Benjamin was getting prepared to use his mind he is sitting on a bench there's a small sound in the back ground he needs total silence not a sound. Benjamin ignores it at first as he focuses as soon he would find himself in a strange place. It was taking him some where. As Benjamin tris to figure himself out it looked like the journey had taken him back street. He was a little bit disappointed but continued a brave move on his account.

He was now sitting down on a bench in the same place that he was in except there ws lots of people as he looked upwards he could hear them.

What sounded like a brushing when I had a second chance to look at it he looked up at me there ws a black guy Benjamin ws having his shoes shined.

Benjamin thought this was a good he knew instantainiously that he was in Fat eds place he also knew exactly why he was there was going to be a robbery and fat Ed was just about to be put out of business and left in some serious debt. Unless Benjamin can re arrange his future. he was trying to figure why it was Eds place there ws plenty of other places he could be, he ws obviously needed. The guy ws filthy rich it would not bother him he would just claim it back in insurance. The shoe shin boy was just filling in Benjamin as he was counting the seconds to the ultimate robbery the casino heist.

Benjamin was confused Benjamin was trying to figure the real reason that he was there the shoe shine boy was telling him Benjamin eyes where else where and misses the most important past of the conversation. This did not help his situation. Benjamin wants in but

also he wants out as he try's the shoe shin boy refuses
to let his foot go as Benjamin is trying to bring himself
back the boy is to talkative for Benjamin's likening.
Benjamin is while trying to figure the real reason why
he is there and trying to get back at the same time.
Benjamin still does not know why he is there.
He closes his eyes everything slows down and
Benjamin enters a room in a room the shoe shine boy
had gone Benjamin knows the score he know knows
why he is there he's playing tonight. Fat ed did not just
own the casino he played the trumpet and pulled a
rather large crowed the only thing he could not pull off
was another line he had women all over him. Within a
few more seconds of being there I got a few more
messages I was in my own future like a good ten years
in to the future. ten years from now it looked like I was
going to make the first move.
I was looking for the times and dates I was checking
out the security and anything that could be of help
especially anything that would explain what I ws doing
there as it had not sunk in to my head. And how I got
away with a robbery. As I looked further in to the future
u could see that I ws going to have some company, I
had some visitors.
The casino was not just being robbed by me but in fact
it was being robbed at the same time by my old street
gang in the future at that time they walked off with the
money this time I ws there to make sure that I walked
off with the money. As I ws just about to find out. As I
filled my bags with the money my other gang walked in
they were still doing the old way they never did things
quietly it had started.
Benjamin:" Who are you".
Gang member:" I could ask you the same question".
Benjamin:" This is my jo, get lost, find your own".

Benjamin continues to fill his sacks. The gang members click on.

Gang members:" Is that you Benjamin".

Benjamin:" Why do you not just yell out my name so the whole world can hear us".

Benjamin tries to make a deal but it all goes wrong they want it all and Benjamin has nothing those were there terms. Benjamin had cleared most of the money in to his sacks. He picks up the bags and prepares himself to go. The man in front of Benjamin is not convinced that it is his old boss.

Gang member:" It is you Benjamin, Benjamin".

The gang member goes for his gun, Benjamin uses the bag as a shield costing Benjamin about half a million as bullets fly and ends up in the air and on then floor scattered the bags were a good enough shield Benjamin and the money that was waisted on the casino volt floor. Benjamin makes his escape but not before sending a message upstairs sending there security down stairs as he disappears. Knowing that he had locked his killer and old gang member and friend behind bars he shouts as Benjamin makes his escape for he second time this evening but does not go far as he needs to see what is going to happen, Benjamin finds a place to hide just so he too can look in to the future to find out how he can escape.

Benjamin is not so surprised as another one of his street gang pal turned up this was the second part of his gang his second posy. The man that we just shot in the safe is dead and now for that you owe us. Benjamin had realized quite quickly that his second posy now called the company had grown they meant serious business. After what Benjamin had just seen he was sacred. He brought himself back straight away the company that killed his old friend were out of control Benjamin knew that this was punishment not business. There were certain rules that we live by all of us we do not just go around making them up they are there for a reason. Benjamin had to remind himself of the rules, and was thinking of them whilst he was thinking of the truth. He awakes finding himself on a park bench in the park it was night time. He wants to go home only to realize that he does not have a home. when he looks down at the floor just thinking about saying something to the heavens he looks down at a shadow thinking nothing of it but when he looks again he puts his hand on something and pulls out after finding a bag handle the bag of money, he is loaded again.

With the smile on his face he heads off somewhere close to the park in town to find a hotel, he was thinking how did he manged to do but he did. He was looking back a seriously stupid thing to do so soon. The security in most casinos was tight filled with officers, and cameras everywhere although in this case it seemed that they had totally forgotten about everything, systems. Walking in was easy apart of wielding two disguises until I got to the volt although not expecting to bump in to my old friends who are now paying the bills and just to top it off I got him kicked and I knew that he would be doing some serious time. The thoughts of the day had lifted my mind like I had lifted the cash and the thought of the cash lift a smile on my face. just another guy that crossed me and through it sent himself down. As I left him behind bars and I know that he had been caught he knew that I was setting him up it was all over his face. I could hear his cry for help but I chose to ignore him.

As I left the casino with no more worry it looked like I had got away with it I had walked out as calmly as I had walked in. tipping the shoe shine boy on the way out.

CHAPTER TWENTY TWO

THREE PLUS TWO EQUELS FIVE

Once I had found a place to stay close to town and near the park I had counted the money that I had stolen from the casino I booked myself straight in to another hotel way out in the country side a place where I could not be disturbed or found. Away from the city. And a good place and safe. Although knowing that I had just set up

Luke it was obvious that he reconised me and he would tell everybody that he had seen me because he had a big mouth. Even more so he ws the only one I the gang who could reconises me from a distance I suppose you could call it he knew my walk. He knew it was me that gave him up to the cops on that dreadful day. I was getting worried that he w as in the same building to k=make an attempt on my life after all he had motive I killed his twin brother. In realaity I knew that he would come looking for me. However The money made up for his presents I was not that worried. I started counting it again just to take my mind off things. I was actually feeling like my old self again. I was feeling like Benjamin.

After a reasonable good sleep for a couple of days I believed that I ws being drawn to my window I did not know what it was but it kept on happening, as it did I was getting more paranoid, it was me I was just thinking that I told myself. With the money I decided to move further in to the country side. I was looking for another hotel as well somewhere away from the old memories hence he arrival of Luke. I could not find one, which up set me. After smashing a few things up in hotel in anger I was asked to leave the hotel, as I was walking still half sober I found myself walking across a field, it was nice and scary but you do not give a shit when you are drunk. I was looking for a hotel I obviously had the directions mixed up. as I came out of the field there was a road, I stepped on to it knowing that I had found hard ground again. It was like being out at sea only to find land. It was a small victory. I closed my eyes as I did there ws total darkness all around me I had crossed over the road to a large field bigger than the previous one. I was on farm land you could smell the manure and you could hear the wild life. If this was farm land there would be a farm house normally reasonably close to it. I kept on walking following he country lanes they were long and they went on for a few miles my concern now was the traffic on the roads and it would be typical if the cops turned up on my way. I had past an odd property and old house it was scarier than the fields and the journey itself.

I had found my way and I was now looking at the houses the question in mind which of the houses was I going to approach. They all had one thing in common it was that they were all old. Even in the country side as for the city life something was telling me the country side was square filled with queer folk. When it come s about being safe. The people were really different they acted hard and looked like they had drowned them selves in cider.

Mind you that did not surprise me, there was apple orchards all over the place. I was looking in my pocket for a cigarette I was lucky I had found one I took the smoke out of the packet holding upwards, I was lucky as it was a new packet and I was surprise that it was there as I thought that I had none. I slipped the smoke in to my mouth. I tugged away on it as I walked in the right direction

The road was winding to the left a lot and there were large hedge fences no room for walkers I ws thanking god that I had not been mowed down, as for luck there ws no traffic.

as I neared the entrance of the farm I was not sure that it was the actual farm house. Although I seemed to be walking in the right direction as the sign posts said. As I entered the farm there were lots of building and I think that it could be easy disturbed. I guess I would have to approach all the building in order to find the rest only to find there bed and breakfast, as I thought off it I did so. You had to be daring to find this place it was hidden I was surprised that anybody was there.

After I was given what I had stole I had another good count, I was ashionsihed that I had five times the amount that I had previously counted I smiled the feeling was incredible obviously a miss count in my defence it was probably the beer thinking about it, it was. Who was I to argue I told myself. The smile on my face got bigger.

It was time to go to the bank except in ws in the middle of the country side and it ws one o'clock in the morning. I knew that I should of just stash the money and I ws in a good place to do that but the thought of losing it was to painful.

I decided to keep the money close to myself for now in wanted it in a bank as quick as possible,

I was excited as I looked at the clock when I looked at the clock in the kitchen it had numbers on it in a strange language. I was thinking that the bank opened at nine o'clock I could not get the waiting feeling off my mind I hated waiting it had that horrible feeling to it I cannot explain. He was thinking that he could be there he just needed to think things over. I was thinking the earlier the better.

Benjamin phones the hotel that he was staying at with what little money he had from before the casino. He pays his bills which ws unusual for him. He makes his way back to town to find the bank which was going to be the hotels. You would think that carrying all that money would be heavy it was. As Benjamin approaches the hotel it is extremely busy people walking a round like mechanical robots. They were like sheep all following each other.

Benjamin was keeping his cool he was waiting just outside the bank which was in the hotel he was talking to himself miming the words come on, he was trying not to think as he was telling himself that he was a customer and not pulling a heist. Eventually one of the staff member turned up, as he is watching her he is thinking that he could actually rob the place it looked nice and quiet anyway that was a thought for the future. Benjamin sighs in relief as the bank doors open, he is the first to walk in. the clerk approaches Benjamin and asks him his business.

Benjamin drops te large black sports bag on to the floor perfectly, looking down on the mat that he is thinking hat he is supposed to be standing on. The clerk welcome Benjamin in. a small conversation starts about the opening of Benjamin's account. Benjamin does not have to do much explaining to convince her that he is genuine all Benjamin's paper work fits his information. Benjamin is taken in to an office where he counts the money with two other clerks that had just arrived. A few hours later Benjamin walks out. Benjamin is told that they would have the paper work to him in a few days, Benjamin agrees what else could he do.

Benjamin is happy and he walks out in to the carpark. Benjamin knows that his luck has changed he is thinking how long will it last. There is always somebody or some thing that happens and it is always him on the receiving end so it may seem.

But for now he is content especially now that he has the money in a bank, Benjamin through all the excitement wants to do it again. Rule number one he remembers not to be too greedy. He was thinking positively and getting more confident about creating a new syndicate. He was off to find what he called was the boys.

Things were looking even better as Benjamin within a week had found himself a knew home the flat again was a upper class penthouse suite he had fallen in love with it as soon as he walked through the doors as he was being shown around he did not need to see the paper work he just agreed with the estate agent and wrote him out a check quickly, everybody was happy. Benjamin had a new home to meditate from.

As the deal as made in the morning it gave Benjamin a chance to settle down and as the evening came he prompted himself and prepared himself for a journey through the mind, the place was fully furnished and Benjamin had sat down on the sofa it was reasonably un comfortable and it felt used. In fact it ws not a sofa as such when Benjamin took a really good look at it, it was a sofa bed. Benjamin looked disappointed. Never the less Benjamin continued. Thinking that at least it was sit able on and not in pieces like the last one. Benjamin's nerves were getting the better of him as he feels a little confusion, he was a little bit out of practice, it had taken him an hour just to prepare himself at first knowing not to fall asleep or it could just turn in to a dream.

He searching for some people on the street, he was watching and following certain people thinking while making precise decisions, in weather or not they were approachable he could tell it ws going to be a long night, I had written down on a piece of card sending them all an invitation to come and work for him. He needed this to work if he wanted the streets back. That was the plan, I was leaving my calling card. It had been a few weeks then I started to receive the calls and within a few hours of that day I had make a hundred cards and half or there about had got back to me approaching me through my mobile phone. I was surprised and happy that the plan I had hidden away in my mind had begun to work. My message was there the streets were about to change.

Word was getting around also that I was creating a new syndicate this did not make things any easier however I guess it would come out eventually. The word was on the street.

As a few weeks went by I had started to interview my new candicate for my new street gang, I had car thief's, drug dealers, robbers, bouncers, runners freshmen and hitmen that was just the boys I will not tell you how many girls I had a lot of them were strippers if you catch my drift. Things were beginning to work again it was not unexpected that I would get a visit from the surrounding gangs in the area. I ws not stupid enough to except there invitation to go and speak with them. it was obvious that they wanted to make a deal. I had left a message on my side as I waiting to hear a answer I was dreaming what could happen in the future I knew that I could find them through my mind but what was the price at that point I did not know. It all counting on the way that they acted.

As more people on the streets began to approach me, I ws losing it I did not realize how popular I was it was criminal that I had never been caught. That is when I met her.

Lucy:" the name is Lucy".

Benjamin:" sorry recruitment is over go away".

Benjamin doe's not look up simply because she is a girl, it ws true the girl looked like she was in he late twenty's. as she is about to leave Benjamin looks up. There was something different about that girl Benjamin can sense something. as Lucy turns away disappointed she turn back and asks Benjamin again.

Benjamin:" No".

But Lucy is positive , Benjamin continues telling her that there is no more room. He apologies again.

Lucy approaches Benjamin as she walks towards him and leans sexy on his desk she tells Benjamin to look up. Benjamin smiles beginning to like he attitude Benjamin continues butting in to stop her conversation.

Lucy gets her message across Benjamin finally compliments her about her attitude as he begins to

question her. Lucy is polite and answers all his
questions honestly. Benjamin explains that honestly
would get her everywhere, He tells her to take a seat.
There ws not one there so she sits down on the floor
Benjamin was quizzing her he thinks she knows what
she is talking about simply by looking at her as she
looked different and sounded different.
Benjamin makes a decision at last and tells her that she
is in. what Benjamin did not know that she wielded the
a same gift as him.
Benjamin closes his eyes and can see her clearly he
jumps backwards in shock he did not expect to see
anything.
Benjamin agrees to let her in as they make an
agreement she is shown the door telling her that he
would be in touch. The girl Lucy is still questioning
Benjamin as she is marched to the front door by
Benjamin when she is thrown out side she sat down by
the door. Benjamin knows that there is something about
her she seemed to stand out. She does not know yet that
she has the gift.
She shouts out to Benjamin through his door Benjamin
opens the door knowing that it was her.

Benjamin knew the girl he believe that they had met before she was the same girl. This ws going all the way back to the start of Benjamin journeys through his mind. They used to ply together teaching each other the way of the mind. Benjamin remembers.

Benjamin stands by his door half open he speaks to the girl.

Benjamin:" look whoever you are I will contact you when I am ready ok now pleas leave".

Lucy:" I cannot".

Benjamin:" Why not everybody else has".

Benjamin's temperament was just about to change. The girl stops him and tells him exactly what is on his mind. She knew what he was thinking.

Benjamin:" How did you know what I was going to say".

Lucy:" because we are one of the same".

Benjamin slams the shut and walks in amazement to his bar he pulls up a stool and sits down on it. Benjamin his now in deep thought thinking, he needs to see the future. he was going to close his eyes there ws a presents behind him. He turns around and the girl is there standing behind him.

Benjamin leans back in shock as he slips backwards off the stool the girl catches him before he falls to the floor.
Benjamin :" Thanks".
Before Benjamin has a chance to finish the sentence Lucy butts in.
Lucy:" That's fine".
Benjamin:" ok I get the picture I have met you before".
Lucy:" you remember".
Benjamin lies.
Benjamin: " No I do not".
Lucy knows that Benjamin was lying.
Lucy:" Look Benjamin you have nothing to worry about whilst I am here".
Benjamin:" I am not, who sent you to me".
LUCY|: I have been here all the time I have been watching you and I have been studying your movements, shall I continue. You are in danger".
Benjamin smiles.
BENJAMIN:" Yeah there is a slight possibility of that of course I have been set up by the syndicate there going to give me what is right fully mine.
LUCY:" You mean the streets".
BENJAMIN:" Yes I mean the streets".
Benjamin and Lucy have connected and Lucy was happy to met Benjamin, as they start to discuss the secrets and the power of there minds Benjamin explains to Lucy tat all the dreams he had were about Lucy. But that in fact as Lucy explains were all real. She new about everything the playing in the fields and the more previous the long walks in to the forest and the fantasy story of the pretend game being in the city of Lou.
BENJAMIN:" You are joking are you not".
LUCY:" No I am not it is all real go on close your eyes".

214

Benjamin reply's to her no Lucy in return insults him
Benjamin still refuses. Lucy continues.

LUCY:" is true you are still a coward".

Within that minute within that sentence both of them
close there eyes and both of them are on the planet they
were in the city of Lou. Benjamin is struggling as the
further he travels in to his mind there were louder
conversations and the harder one s were just arriving.
Lucy was backing Benjamin was busy losing control it
was to powerful for his mind. He bows out Lucy does
the same. They met together and discuss exactly what
happened.

LUCY:" Do not worry it takes a lot of practice you will
pick it up again eventually".

Benjamin just looks at her and then tells her that he
needs time to think. He leaves the kitchen area were
they were standing talking and he walks in to his
lounge. It was a little more relaxing there, he opens the
large windows which look like large glass doors. he
takes a deep breath of fresh air. Lucy being Lucy
follows him.

BENJAMIN:" Now what I think that I have failed".

LUCY:" Not as such it takes a lot of power it will come
you as we practice remember there are two of us now
so yes it would feel a little different you will get used to
it, it can work both ways you either make it or won't
make it in this case you did not make it so we will try
again like I said it will take time just like everything".

BENJAMIN:" It is tiring I am actually tired".

LUCY:" You can be like I said you will get used to it".
Benjamin answers sarcastically.

LUCY:" I am not from your world Benjamin".

Benjamin did not hear her as he lays down on his sofa
within a few minutes he had fallen asleep. Happy and
content that Lucy was there to guard him.

215

CHAPTER TWENTY THREE

RUNNING OUT OF TIME

As Benjamin and Lucy start there relationship again
and Lucy had become Benjamin s teacher the in and out
of mind power was the subject. They were busy
discussing energy and the way it works. At this point
they were questioning where it comes from. It was a
seriously different conversation that Benjamin was used
to or to be in. Benjamin ws the question answering
question after question in the end Lucy gave in trying to
teach him and in the end told him to close his eyes
continuing that we will try it the old fashioned way. He
did as Lucy had asked, They were going to do it Lucy's
way.

Just as Benjamin was going to try and answer a
question that Lucy had given him she tells him to shut
his mouth. Benjamin doe's so with a smile. Lucy
retrieve a load of knowledge from her old memory this
was going to take some time she did not tell him that it
would take a couple of days depending on how
intelligent that Benjamin was. Lucy begin s the process.
Lucy is running out of time. It was a dangerous thing to
attempt as if she makes one mistake as she process and
transfers the knowledge she could lose her self in her
self and totally end up a completely different   person.

And Lucy would have to find her way back to Benjamin into Benjamin. She ws explaining that and it sound stupid for example she could end up in a totally different place or in a different country with different people with a different mind. Benjamin speaks out he is talking I his sleep.

BENJAMIN:" I heard that".

LUCY:" Heard what".

BENJAMIN:" What did you say if you lose your way".

LUCY:" That is good Benjamin that is a bonus that shows that it is working now please be quiet I'm working I am trying to concentrate".

As Lucy takes him to the second stage, Benjamin tells Lucy to keep going the sensation he said was incredible. And she would not believe the things that he was seeing. Lucy explains it is knowledge. Then all of a sudden there was silence, nothing then Lucy speaks. Telling Benjamin to stay put do not speak just yet, Benjamin was still asleep he stays silent Lucy could see that he was amazed with the knowledge that he had just received. Now they could move forward. He told that it felt really good after he had awoke.

Not knowing exactly what had happened to himself Benjamin comes over in a hot sweat then cold. His temperature was off the scales and his persistent swearing ws also a problem. It was cool with Lucy she took it as side affects she ws just s9iting on the break fast table feet off the ground and her arms at her sides. As Benjamin walks around his home he needs the space to pace acting totally out of character. Saying things he did not mean and focused on Lucy.

LUCY:" Do not worry in a minute and a half you will come back to normal, but you will sleep for a few hours as what we just did has a side effect. In fact it has two". Benjamin looks up and passes out again not on the furniture but on the floor.

Lucy continues.

LUCY:" One you are already experiencing".

Benjamin had not past out totally and answers Lucy quietly.

BENJAMIN:" Well thanks for telling me". As Benjamin gets up only to fall over again this time missing the floor and landing on his couch.

Those were Benjamin last words of Benjamin. As Lucy plays around having fun moving the body around as Benjamin did not look to comfortable laying were he was laying. She runs his dianostic heart rate, blood, and temperature and pulse, everything is well considering. She was happy that Benjamin was alive. Lucy goes into the kitchen to find him some coffee as she is timing everything. Lucy speaks to Benjamin being cheeky knowing that he can not hear her.

LUCY:" I hope you do mind but I am having a cup of coffee".

Benjamin is sound asleep Lucy wants to know if he is dreaming there ws no way of knowing and she was temped to enter his mind while he sleeps. But she waits as there would be plenty of chances to do that in the near future. she sits down on the other side of the room watching him sleep he was there and would be there for hours. It could be days depending on how his brain works and how his mind will work as he a just s to the knowledge that he a has just received. Benjamin was speaking I his sleep again Lucy chooses to listen to him but ignores as a dream he did not say anything that was important too her or effects him in the future. she agreed with her self to question him later she planed to do this the next time they were to talk.

Benjamin was out cold still twelve hours this meant that the knowledge was surrounding his brain.

And what is left would take over his body and mind. The real question was why ws she doing this who was the girl looking for a life of crime was this revenge or purely that she was board which one brought her to Benjamin's home this does not mean that she wants to be in Benjamin's new syndicate

Why was she doing this.

She knows that Benjamin has made himself enough partners in his business to start his firm off. Thanks to a robbery everybody wins with the rest of the money that ws brought in from other crimes everybody was flush and it was on Benjamin. This time Benjamin watches every move that is made he watches everything that comes in and everything that goes out. And he is watching everybody including the cops. When he wakes up he is not sure the things that he had seen were real if they were going to happen or that they were happening the presents of the girl was not helping his situation although he was polite enough not to question her yet. There was a colder felling in his home he did not like but he still opens the window to let the fresh air in.

Benjamin had received images from everywhere he was getting phone calls every couple of minutes he had to turn off his phone for a break. There was a knock at Benjamin's door as he tells the person on the other end of the phone call that he would call them back, he opens the door and knows the four men at the door. He asks them in continuing his phone call.

BENJAMIN:" Yeah just do it doe's not matter, if you make a mess just do not leave any prints and keep your masks on at all times".

Two thugs:" We have your goods".

BENJAMIN:" Good just leave it on the table". He points to one of the members of his gang tells him to wait as he gets another phone call. After Benjamin puts the phone down after speaking quickly and quietly he puts his phone down. Benjamin tells the man to count the money he can go after he had finished.

Things were running nicely for Benjamin he ws back to his old ways the syndicate was running he had made enough money it was time he had a few friend s to VISIT pay back time.

I had already killed three of my old gang, companions I
suppose you could call them, mate's that were closer
than class mates, reason, they were not to loyal to be
part of the grind syndicate. As knew members formed
new gangs steeling friends from me with bribes and
more money I was losing my posy again this saddened
me knowing that some people on there list were like
family to me. I am not the father I was just wealthy
through crime a business man with a lot of connections.
I had three of my boys or what ever you would call
them I do not know thugs, except I prefer to deal with
my personal problems myself. I was on one end of the
gun he was son the other it was a good job that I was
holding it form the right end, it was a quick and easy
removal, not to much blood it was straight a couple of
bullets to his knees he would never walk again.

As most of the pub ran out it was his drinking hole I ws
left alone with the screams and cry's of it customers
and his cry's of pain.
BENJAMIN:" I'll have a whisky".
BARMAN:" Yeah sure".
The barman did not seems to be bothered it probably
happens in his place all the time. The barman slides the
whisky bottle down the bar it was something out of a
western. Benjamin took on notice of him he was not in
the mood of being entertained he ws hardly amused.
BENJAMIN:" Are you being funny".
The barman realizes that Benjamin meant business
Benjamin asks the barman for another drink this time

he puts the glass in front of Benjamin and pours him drink. When Benjamin shows him his gun as he asks him what's in the till. The barman understood Benjamin, Benjamin tells him again he wants the bar takings. The bar man give Benjamin all the money in the till, including the coins. Benjamin asks him for another drink, Benjamin pays the barman from the money that he had stolen no notes just penny's. The barman draws himself a shot. Meantime the man on the floor had stopped shouting and finally gets Benjamin s attention as this is happening as the man is crawling out of the building towards the doors, Benjamin continues to drink.

He thanks the barman for his hospitality he shoots the man on the floor as he reaches the door. Benjamin makes his way over the body and to his car.

BENJAMIN:" All done lets go before the whole town knows that we have been here".

Benjamin and his two friends are in the car discussing weather it would be a good idea to kill there next target and kill two bird s with one stone. They agreed that it would be possible in one night. Benjamin disagrees and says it would be impossible because there would be two many of there men he reminds them that the guy that he had just killed will be found Benjamin continues I bet the bar man is on the phone right now as we speak. Benjamin continues they will be coming to us Benjamin new in a couple of days it would be all over the street. Both of the gangs had ears everywhere. Benjamin has told his people invent a message as wall have ears too. Benjamin was challenging and changing the message, making out that it ws some other posy and he had nothing to do with it. his message went out. He would not be contempt until he hears his own words. Eventually it was done it ws made out to be a gang killing possibly from abroad, Benjamin believes that he ahs got away with it. At that moment he realizes that fat ed would figure it out within a few month the blame was on the syndicate, Benjamin actions were not taken lightly on the street.

Benjamin was finding things different and weird on the street so many people had disappeared names of clubs changing Benjamin always had this saying the street names never change there are always the same. Good for the postman bad if your doing a runner or should I say on the end of a chance. The experiences that Benjamin had ion the street as a teenager was all coming back. He believes that he is being called upon again. He stops what he is doing, this time it ws a little more serious as people were dying. It was not particularly breaking his heart to know that somebody ws out there killing his friends the same people he trusted twenty years ago. People he trusted walking out he trusted them only to be destroyed by his closes friends and it was all through his decisions. He was running it then and he was running it again. In fact he had been running his entire life he did not know after everything that had happened he would end up in this position that he ws now back in.

Benjamin has to think he ws lying to himself about his life and he was ignoring the fact that he had a choice but to except it thinking about it was slowly becoming Benjamin's sickness even though he had never been caught.

After sitting down after receiving the knowledge of her entire mind I was in my chair behind my desk it had felt good for a few hours however she had told me what to expect and what ws to come next. The first thing that was going to happen was extremely painful it was called a bullet for the simple reason it felt like taking one the only way it could be stopped was when the girl decided to stop it. the pain was incredible Benjamin in all of the pain needed to patch a few things up it was that painful. He had broken a few things in the kitchen that he could easily be replace as the pain went on he went on damaging other things trying to avoid the most expensive things in his apartment. Benjamin had to slam his hand down hard so that he could avoid breaking the extremely expensive painting on his kitchen wall. The next thing came to Benjamin unexpectedly. She through something at Benjamin he catches it the item it was an eye patch she tells him to put it on.

BENJAMIN:" What is this for".

LUCY:" Just put it on".

BENJAMIN:" what".

LUCY:" Just put the eye patch on I think it would suit you".

Benjamin throws it back to her Benjamin insists that his vision is fine Lucy smiles and they begin to talk.

Either way what was done was done even if it could change the past I would not it seemed a little shelf fish . It was all quiet again and the girl wanted to speak to me again I was trying to tell her that I did not want to be approached at this moment. She ws not listening this time she waited until it was late in the evening. I did not stop to question her I just walked past her. A conversation started.

BENJAMIN:" What are you doing here I told you not to follow me and I will call you when I need you".

LUCY:" Err you did invite me".

BENJAMIN:" Who do you work for".

LUCY:" You I work for you".

BENJAMIN:" I do not know you do I".

LUCY:" Yes you do you have known of me for year and years ".

Benjamin was just about to find out that Lucy ws not Lucy but she was a computerised image Benjamin was just starting to lose his mind.

BENJAMIN:" Go away go you are not real go away go back go home go where the hell did you come from "

LUCY:" I came from your mind, I came from the future".

As Benjamin slowly realizes that he is in big trouble and this occurrence would change everything especially if his syndicate find s out it would totally destroy everything that that he had worked for. Right now he was on top of his business. Benjamin is in shock and he wants to question her.

BENJAMIN:" Who else knows".

LUCY:" Knows what".

BENJAMIN:" Knows about me and you".

LUCY:" Nobody".

BENJAMIN:" Can any body else see you".

LUCY:" That depends on how much money you are willing to give me. and how much you give me for being quiet".

BENJAMIN:" Are you trying to bribe me that's good how much were you thinking off"

LUCY:" Nothing wait there is a pause your thinking how about your soul".

BENJAMIN:" I was waiting for that one".

LUCY:" Maybe you would like me to repeat it what me I do not do the holy thing in fact quite the opposite, sometimes, however in saying that your quite a character do you still like me".

Benjamin end s the conversation with a large echoing scream.

BENJAMIN:" Go away".

Benjamin is confused about his new situation and he was trying to figure out was the girl really real or was she part of his imagination Benjamin dreams about her all day he still does not figure it out that the girl is a electronic computerized hallucination he keeps on dreaming into the night. Hardly sleeping as the thought of her was keeping him awake. Benjamin was cracking up over the situation that he was in. The best thing that Benjamin could do for now is switch himself off.

As the morning arrived Benjamin through lack of sleep felt even more sick he was not used to missing his sleep although his symptoms did not show and he was not really that bad. He walks slowly and casually to his bath room. It was cold and dark as he had no lightbulb in the light socket, unusual for Benjamin as his home was normally perfect everything in it's place. Benjamin strips down to his waist he picks up the bar of soap half used and left on the bath room sink top. He turns on the water cold not hot that was unusual too. At that point he did not care, as the tap was running, he bows his head putting himself in to position down and forwards using his hand to splash the cold water on to his face. then once nice and wet rubbing in the soap on his and s then his face as he does he speaks to himself taking him through the steps as he washed. Believing that he was by himself he continues to talk his words were at the end of the conversation were crime pays as he moves his head upwards looking into the mirror he jumps back in shock as the girl is there that answers his conversation. He was thinking that was a quick answer to long conversation that he does not want he shouts. Benjamin knows that he is running out of time this time he ignores the girl it clear to him that it was Lucy. It was just another day in the life of Benjamin. Lucy picks up the towel whi9ch she hands to Benjamin and Benjamin takes it and dry's himself after he is done he puts the towel down on the towel rail. Lucy then implies that Benjamin is in a good mood he ignores the conversation and does not answer her. He walks out of the bathroom in to the kitchen his kitchen is not small as Benjamin looks around forgetting what he is looking for then he recovers his thoughts reaching up in to a cubboard and pulling out a jar of coffee, putting down gently on the side not forgetting the milk he goes to his fridge and opens the door slowly pulling a small carton of milk out and placing by the coffee jar. He can see the girl and is watching her carefully as she follows his movements, and when Benjamin stops she stops this continued through out the day. As Benjamin picks up his coffee the girl pretends to do the same eventually at the end Benjamin tells her to stop after she repeats the sentence back to him she stops this continued all day and it did not stop until Benjamin loses his temper. A few minutes after Benjamin had his out burst the girl disappears.

Benjamin thinks that he is talking to something holy also thinking that it could be the other way around he closes his eyes to see what's going on in his world of Benjamin he takes control almost immediately as he takes control of his street business. He is watching his boys.

Benjamin was there for a few hours he was happy with what he has seen and with the progress that he had made. He ws happy that the syndicate was running things for him. At that point he things were looking good and he had no complaints. Benjamin was thinking he knows that he's in trouble, he knows that he can not afford to lose the syndicate or that the syndicate loses there faith in him. After he had done a few more weeks Benjamin was looking a little rough people in the syndicate and on the street had started talking, it was happening all over again. In all the frustrations Benjamin locks himself away, for a few weeks which turned in to months on top of that Lucy was still around paying him a visit. Benjamin would be talking, his main man would be asking the questions Benjamin would say he was just expressing his mind.

He continues all in a day's work as he jokes to his body guard. Benjamin knows that he is cracking up. he knows that he could not hide the truth forever. But insisted to himself that he would not give in and he would try.

As another week past in mind Benjamin was looking like he was in a mess. He had been living on take away and he wanted some proper grub. He calls to his body guard and tells him to bring the car around the front, it was quite usual for Benjamin to use a driver he like it because it would cause a stir and bring more attention to him. He would also walk as he knew the streets and he liked the night time. How ever at this time he decided that he wanted to be driven only for the fact of what had occurred in his mind. Simply for the fact that it was also exercise and that he could gat some fresh air. Rather than inhaling air in his home which was not air as for all the smoking that he does. He was pretty much a chain smoker he put it down to pressure. On the way back he decided to go to a restaurant. It was the usual scene the restaurant was packed solid. It was unusual for Benjamin to wait but on this occasion. The receptionist finally calls him after half an hour.
Receptionist:" Hello sir sorry about the wait please come this way we have a table for you".

Before the waiter can offer more of his services Benjamin orders his usual the waiter writes it all down at the end even before the waiter had asked Benjamin if there was anything else Benjamin had ordered him self his bottle of wine.

As Benjamin walked around the filled restaurant it felt weird instead of walking round he tried to walk through that was his mistake as all the tables were close together as I turned around to make my way back I noticed that things had changed and it had. As I finally found my table and was seated I noticed again that it was close to the fire exit that did not help with the paranoia to be honest it was not that comfortable at first but I got used to it. the table was neatly clothed with a large white table cloth and there was a wine bucket on the middle of the table. In the table amongst the plates and three wine bottles unopened. Benjamin was just saying to him self that he could get used to this, then he heard it the girl turned up.

Benjamin looks upwards rubbing his hands over his face thinking not now almost straight away she started talking Benjamin just tells her to go away. she ignores Benjamin's request and continues to question him. As a conversation starts more and more people begin to turn there heads as Benjamin his having a conversation to an image that only he can see. it looks like Benjamin is talking to himself.

His last words that evening was something like thanks a lot Lucy.

Benjamin hands are on his head as for missing the rules again he calls the waiter over. Lucy had disappeared again only to come back as the waiter, Benjamin did not notice sat first until he heard his voice.

LUCY:" Tip please".

Benjamin knows that she is joking and tells her to shove off, when he looks up the waiter is the waiter. Benjamin appoligises as he reached in to his wallet he tips the waiter exactly two pounds after he pays his bill. Benjamin leaves the restaurant before he is asked to leave by the boss as he loses his temper with Lucy Benjamin believe s that he is the only person that could see her and yet has to ask her if she can be seen by other people. This makes things even more complicated.

Benjamin is sitting at his table hoping that he did not draw to much attention to himself after the out burst the conversation with Lucy he was now apologising for his behaviour as it looked to the other guests like Benjamin was having a conversation with himself. Either way he had turned a few heads once it had stopped and the conversation was still going on as the waiter was waiting Benjamin calms the guests and makes some excuses and lightly jokes that he had just split up with his wife. Benjamin wipes his mouth with a napkin and pushes it away with his plate which was on the table then pulls it back in to his lap. He gets up not pushing the chair back wards leaving the napkin on the table with his plate he walks out of the restaurant. A few minutes later the guests in the restaurant could still hear Benjamin as he can still see Lucy he shouts loudly at her although Benjamin thinks it meant nothing and was still acting like she was not there. Benjamin could hear the rest of the people in the restaurant cheer this did not impress him in fact it made him feel worse.

After leaving the restaurant he is greeted by two of his boys, Benjamin asks them what they are doing they told Benjamin that they were watching over him he asks them why totally losing his temper as he shouts if I needed protection I would ask for protection he grabs one of the young lads by the ear then says to the other your lucky both of you in my office he pushes the pair tomorrow morning do not be late, the boys thought that they were doing him a favour as it happens it was quite the opposite. Benjamin gets I to his car, he says to his driver that he would be doing the driving this evening with a smile on his face , as he pushes the keys in to the ignition he puts the car in gear and drives off. Sloley as the boy that he man handled was getting up Benjamin shouts to them get the train home. his words were loud as the second boy helps pick up his partner Benjamin shouts again nine pm do not be late. As this happens the girl appears again Benjamin was already speeding and she insists that that he should slow down but by then it was to late the old bill that 's the police pull him over as this happens he is already in conversation with Lucy. He finally calms down as the police just get there as the officer steps towards the drivers side of the car. Benjamin knows the score and just as there was a police man present he did not change his attitude the police man tells Benjamin to relax as he taps on the window as Benjamin un winds the window there conversation ws a short one Benjamin's argument was that he was in the speed limit the officer disagrees and tells Benjamin that he was doing well over forty in the forty zone, Benjamin is handed a ticket he knows the rest he drops the ticket on purpose he was temped to bump the officer.

Officer:" do you take me for a fool">

This made things even more harder on Benjamin.

Benjamin:" No officer".

Officer:" then get out of the car and pickup your ticket".

BENJAMIN:" Er".

Benajmin hesitates.

BENJAMIN:" Just write me another one".

The officer again tells Benjamin to get out of the car and pick up his ticket. After a few minutes Benjamin does so, the police men turn away, Lucy appears again Benjamin speaks using dirty language the police man stops and turns around.

Officer:" excuse me but what did you just say".

Benjamin insists that he has said nothing the officer wants Benjamin to get out of the car. Benjamin tells him and insists that he has done nothing wrong and persisted in his innocent that he has done nothing wrong. an argument starts and of course the officer wins. As Benjamin is asked to give up his keys at first he denies it and refuses and try's to appoligises. The police now believe that he is hiding something. the argument continues even further Benjamin tries to explain that he was just on his way home. and he was still content in saying that he was under the limit when they pulled him over. Benjamin finally gets out of his car in all the frustrations he loses his temper there was a few good explicit words given from Benjamin to the officer. Who knew that he was going to arrest him Benjamin was wishing his boys were around and argues while arguing about he understood why they were following him. What a mistake Benjamin thought. As the police man ws writing the conversation all down.

Benjamin snaps what are you doing the police man insists that Benjamin keeps his distance and cool, and explains that he is being arrested Benjamin can not believe it he closes the windows and locks all of the doors he is forced to give the policemen his car keys on doing that he sees Lucy again she is dressed like a cop Benjamin is not amused Benjamin was asking himself if he was going insane Lucy speaks to Benjamin telling him to plead total insanity. With that Benjamin smiles as his head is ducked in to the back of the police car. After fifteen minutes and issued a speeding ticket and told if he does not pay within a week he would be going to court. Benjamin was free to go.

CHAPTER TWENTY FOUR

DO NOT TURN UP

Benjamin finally gets home everything is quiet he is smiling on the evening events, those kind of things make Benjamin feel big, another laugh for his syndicate to talk about. He thought as he looked around there was nothing to see. He felt a great sign of relief on the real side of things, and not understating his situation the reality of the whole situation. He never used to think about it being such a sane teenager. As he remembers as he is lying down on his sofa thinking. There is a knock on the door he checks his phone knowing that he was not expecting any body as he gets up he turns off the lights in the living room and in his hall way as he walks through his cooridoor up to the front door he looks through the spy hole he sees nothing and thinks it a prank as he turns away to walk back to his lounge the door bell rings again this time he is closer he looks through the spy hole again and again he see nothing. He waits a moment then opens the door, it was Lucy. Lucy did not even ask him in she just walked right past him and walked in. it was like he was not there Benjamin knows that she is a little bit cocky he follows

237

her to his kitchen she makes her self a cup of coffee.
Benjamin is busy talking his joke was that she was so
flamboyant that she should of offered her self a beer,
she was being cheeky.
Benjamin snatches the coffee out of her hand and pours
the cup of coffee down his sink as he turns around she
is going through the fridge. He is disgruntled and has
that expression on his face as she takes him for a beer
from his four pack. As she opens it Benjamin agrees to
himself that he has lost. Lucy starts to talk about
yesterdays late evening events Benjamin just wants her
to leave him and gives her some verbal abuse Lucy is
not listening, Benjamin wanted a beer as well he refers
to her like being his wife and he says she acted lie they
had an affair the both of them. one minute laughing and
the next arguing. Benjamin was glad that he did not
have any children he gives her no reasons and it ws
clear that he was motivated by money. Benjamin is
trying not to talk to talk her as she walks around the
apartment going from room to room Benjamin is trying
his hardest not to talk to her, or even answer her back.
Benjamin closes his eyes it was easier what Benjamin
did not realize he was supposed to be thinking of her.
He had totally forgotten.as he thought of it he kept it to
himself.

Although saying thank you to her which was ignored she simply did not want to go away. Benjamin realizes that he has a gift, as he looks at his situation he is beginning to think that it was not that bad. Maybe she would eventually leave if he spoke to it. Benjamin was being optimistic he was thinking that it be a good thing and he might be able to use her for his own use he was thinking that he could use her to his advantage.

Benjamin was going to try out his new theory he wants to know if he can get in to Lucy's mind. He closes his eyes and makes the first attempt, he gets no reaction form her he got nowhere as he opens his eyes Lucy is no where to be seen. And especially nowhere to be heard.

Benjamin knows that he cannot live the rest of his life in darkness of his own mind, but closing his eyes for an hour seemed to draw her closer to him it was distracting and she had reappeared. Quite unusual Benjamin thought, and goes to work on the new theory. Later on in the evening Lucy appears again Benjamin closes his eyes and again she disappears. This is good Benjamin believes he had found one answer and wants to find others. Benjamin sits down after shouting at Lucy. As she appears to him again as he forgets to close his eyes this time he remembers just as Lucy was going to speak. This time she is talking about his business the syndicate. As Benjamin listens to her the girl Lucy is telling him how things have changed and how they are going to happen. If he listens to her, she ws looking for a confession. In the end he closes his eyes again wishing her away. she disappears but not after she tells Benjamin that the boys had doubled crossed him for the third time, Benjamin thinks about what Lucy had said. A string of thought run through Benjamin s mind Benjamin wants to see the future, he was feeling desperate and started to act like it. Lucy was enjoying watching him sweat.

As he closes his eyes for a few minutes which turned in to hours he had found his gift again he was in control again he ws in control of his syndicate Benjamin is watching the docks. Some of the boys were cashing in on his deals the girl ws right she was not lying. The deal that they were making with out Benjamin was a weapon deal. His mind then moves away he finds himself in town he can not make out the images but it felt like a couple of his lads were pulling off a bank job. He ws glad to see them hard at work.

The next lot of boys were pulling off a jewlery store, dimonds and gold Benjamin after he had seen that was feeling rich. it had been a while since he had seen his boys he was happy but still concerned over Lucy, Benjamin knew that she was not going to go and she would be there for the rest of his life. He closes his eyes once more to watch the last of his jobs the girl interrupts, Benjamin ignores her she is trying to tell him that he had some visitors Benjamin did not listen and did not answer the door the girl Lucy was right Benjamin knew that it could be trouble as his syndicate knew not to approach him with out an invitation. He checks his phone to check his messages. No messages. That must be trouble he asks Lucy to tell him who is at the door, Lucy refuses to answer Benjamin asks her again and again Lucy refuses to answer Benjamin knows that he has to answer the door himself ass he gets up but before he has a chance to get there to the front door the large door is forced open the police thee everywhere and they are quick there was somebody shouting Benjamin is thrusted over on to the floor in his hallway cuffed and arrested.

Police officer:" Ok os5 turn the hologram off we have our man".

Benjamin:" a hologram I have been watching a hologram".

Police officer:" Yeah that's right, we have been watching you for a very long time Benjamin and we have been waiting for you for this very day ever since I met you on the play ground.

Benjamin is put into a car he knows that he is going to jail Benjamin knows not to say a word. Benjamin is feeling a little emotional. He was really fighting the tears as they feel from his eyes he knew that his time was over as he pulled his hanky out to dry his tears from his jacket pocket as he wiped away the last tear it was a single one long. He puts the hanky back into his jacket pocket. Benjamin is already planning to run. If you did not know the streets well it meant that he what's to escape. However on this occasion the doors on the car were locked extremely well. Benjamin is still thinking and he now wants some fresh air the coppers were not buying it. As Benjamin is finding his arrest a little hard to think about. Eventually he realizes that he is not going anywhere, he was now th8nking about his sanity that's the only part of himself that he cared about.

The police car pulls up, Benjamin presumed that he was going to the police station but he finds himself with the police in a police car in a car park at the end of some street I suppose you could call it waist land. The two cops get out of the car taking Benjamin with them. Benjamin knows this is not good, they tell him to start walking, Benjamin knows that it was a hit. He did not stand a chance, unarmed and in the open with no where

to run and no cover. He was counting his steps as he walked he falls on to his knees there is aloud sounds of guns being fired, Benjamin is dead.
Eliminated, assassinated his body laid on the cold concrete floor the police men call it in Benjamin takes his last breath alone and he dies alone.